"I don't believe my job description mentions anything about marriage," Kate said.

Richard reached over and patted her hand. "Relax. We'll get married, but we won't really be married. We'll go through with a ceremony for Mrs. Delacroix's benefit, but we'll skip all the legal requirements."

She knew he hadn't been sincere about marrying her, of course, but hearing him speak of it so dismissively rankled all the same. "You're taking an awful lot for granted, aren't you? What makes you think I'll go along with a crazy scheme like this?"

"I know it's asking a lot, but will you help me out?"

Kate's head warned her she was making a drastic mistake, but her heart gave her no other option. The heat of Richard's imploring gaze melted the last shred of her already weakened resistance.

Swallowing hard, she slowly nodded.

Dear Reader,

July brings you the fifth title of Silhouette Romance's VIRGIN BRIDES promotion. This series is devoted to the beautiful metaphor of the traditional white wedding and the fairy-tale magic of innocence awakened to passionate love on the wedding night. In perennial favorite Sandra Steffen's offering, *The Bounty Hunter's Bride,* a rugged loner finds himself propositioned by the innocent beauty who'd nursed him to health in a remote mountain cabin. He resists her precious gift...but winds up her shotgun groom when her father and four brothers discover their hideaway!

Diana Whitney returns to the Romance lineup with *One Man's Promise,* a wonderfully warmhearted story about a struggling FABULOUS FATHER and an adventurous single gal who are brought together by their love for his little girl and a shaggy mutt named Rags. And THE BRUBAKER BRIDES are back! In *Cinderella's Secret Baby,* the third book of Carolyn Zane's charming series, tycoon Mac Brubaker tracks down the poor but proud bride who'd left him the day after their whirlwind wedding, only to discover she's about to give birth to the newest Brubaker heir....

Wanted: A Family Forever is confirmed bachelor Zach Robinson's secret wish in this intensely emotional story by Anne Peters. But will marriage-jaded Monica Griffith and her little girl trust him with their hearts? Linda Varner's twentieth book for Silhouette is book two of THREE WEDDINGS AND A FAMILY. When two go-getters learn they must marry to achieve their dreams, a wedding of convenience results in a *Make-Believe Husband*...and many sleepless nights! Finally, a loyal assistant agrees to be her boss's *Nine-to-Five Bride* in Robin Wells's sparkling new story, but of course this wife wants her new husband to be a *permanent* acquisition!

Enjoy each and every Silhouette Romance!

Regards,

Joan Marlow Golan

Joan Marlow Golan
Senior Editor Silhouette Books

Please address questions and book requests to:
Silhouette Reader Service
U.S.: 3010 Walden Ave., P.O. Box 1325, Buffalo, NY 14269
Canadian: P.O. Box 609, Fort Erie, Ont. L2A 5X3

NINE-TO-FIVE BRIDE

Robin Wells

Silhouette
R O M A N C E™
Published by Silhouette Books
America's Publisher of Contemporary Romance

To Ken, my round-the-clock husband

SILHOUETTE BOOKS

ISBN 0-373-19311-4

NINE-TO-FIVE BRIDE

Copyright © 1998 by Robin Rouse Wells

Printed in U.S.A.

ROBIN WELLS

Before becoming a full-time writer, Robin was a hotel public relations executive whose career ran the gamut from writing and producing award-winning videos to organizing pie-throwing classes taught by circus clowns. At other times in her life she has been a model, a reporter and even a charm school teacher. But her life-long dream was to become an author, a dream no doubt inspired by having parents who were librarians and who passed on their love of books.

Robin lives just outside New Orleans with her husband and two young daughters, Taylor and Arden. Although New Orleans is known as America's Most Romantic City, Robin says her personal romantic inspiration is her husband, Ken.

Robin is an active member of the Southern Louisiana chapter of the Romance Writers of America. Her first book won RWA's national 1995 Golden Heart Award.

When she's not writing, Robin enjoys gardening, antiquing, discovering new restaurants and spending time with her family. Robin loves to hear from readers and can be reached at P.O. Box 303, Mandeville, LA 70470-0303.

Kate's favorite tips

from

FROMBY'S GUIDE TO CONJUGAL BLISS

1. Frequent marital relations are the key to a blissful union.

2. It is the wife's duty to regularly ignite, stoke and extinguish the fires of her husband's desire.

3. The wise husband continually woos his wife with affectionate gestures and unexpected gifts.

4. Every husband needs an occasional reminder that other men find his wife attractive.

5. Every wife longs to hear the verbal expression of her husband's love and adoration.

6. To maintain an aura of excitement, the wise wife keeps her husband constantly guessing what she'll do next.

Chapter One

"My late husband always said I had good instincts about people." Mrs. Delacroix leaned forward over the gilt-edged desk that dominated her Pepto-Bismol-pink office and batted her false eyelashes at the man seated beside Kate on the velvet love seat. "And my instincts about you, Mr. Chandler, are most favorable."

Kate stared down at her steno pad to hide her grin. Mrs. Delacroix was old enough to be Richard's grandmother, but the flamboyant old gal was flirting with him all the same.

Not that she should be surprised, Kate thought wryly. During the eight months she'd worked as Richard Chandler's secretary, she'd seen woman after woman fall victim to his charm. She herself was less than immune to it. Far less immune than she would have liked, she thought glumly, sneaking a peek at the tall, handsome man beside her and feeling her insides flip-flop in an all-too-familiar surge of attraction—especially since he didn't even seem aware she was female.

But then, Richard's taste in women ran to tall, leggy blondes with impressive bustlines and even more impressive social connections. Kate's hair was dark and curly, her figure was short and slight, and the closest thing to a social registry containing her name was the Greater New Orleans phone directory. She knew she wasn't a candidate for a starring role in an Alpo commercial, but she wasn't Richard Chandler's type, either.

And he wasn't hers, she quickly reminded herself—never mind that his smile turned her bones to Liquid Paper and his eyes made her heart race faster than her fingers on a computer keyboard. She wanted a man who believed in lasting love and marriage, not a man who went through women like courses at a fine French Quarter restaurant—one at a time, but in rapid succession.

Besides, her idea of husband material didn't extend to men who lived, breathed and probably even dreamed of business conquests. Richard approached life as if it were a math equation that could always be solved by effort and logic. He probably didn't have a genuinely sentimental bone in his body. Even the women he dated were selected with an eye to what business contacts they could facilitate or how they might otherwise assist him in his never-ending pursuit of acquiring, revitalizing and reselling failing companies.

No, although he exuded a gravitational pull on every female within eyesight and had a smile that could charm the raisins out of an oatmeal cookie, Richard Chandler wasn't the type of man *she* would ever get involved with. Kate wanted a marriage like the one her parents had shared until the day they'd died—loving, close, caring, committed—and Richard had no use for marriage at all. She'd frequently heard him refer to it as an emotional black hole. And when she'd taken a vacation day last month to help plan her best friend's wedding, Richard had remarked that she'd be doing her friend a bigger favor if she'd spent the day talking her out of it.

Kate had been shocked. "What on earth do you mean?"

"Marriage is like suicide—it's a permanent solution to a temporary situation. All relationships eventually burn themselves out."

"They most certainly do not! What about all the people who stay married for a lifetime?"

Richard had shrugged. "Some people have an unusually high tolerance for misery."

No question about it, she and Richard were completely incompatible; so the wise course of action was to keep her thoughts off his personal assets and on the benefits of her job. It was a job that offered many, Kate reminded herself: exciting challenges, constant change and twice the salary she'd earned at her previous position at a small insurance agency in Ohio.

Kate turned her attention back to Mrs. Delacroix just as the old woman gave Richard a coy grin. It was discouraging to note that even advanced age didn't confer any resistance to his appeal, Kate thought disheartenedly.

"You strike me most favorably indeed, Mr. Chandler," Mrs. Delacroix repeated, her pearl earrings sweeping against cheeks that were so plump, wrinkled and heavily rouged they reminded Kate of baked apples.

Richard flashed one of the smiles that always made Kate's pulse flutter. This time was no exception. "Does that mean you're willing to sell me your hotel?"

The elderly lady's hand flitted from her improbably blond hair to the collar of her pink silk dress—an outfit that, Kate suspected, had been selected to complement the cloyingly pink walls of her office. With its spindly-legged furnishings, fringed lamp shades and elaborately framed paintings of Renaissance nudes, it looked more like a bordello boudoir than a hotel business office.

Everything about the woman gave new meaning to the term *colorful character,* Kate thought with amusement. Yet despite the fact her own tastes were diametrically opposed to Mrs. Delacroix's, she'd taken an immediate liking to the elderly lady.

Mrs. Delacroix flicked her preposterous eyelashes at Richard again. "I must say, it would certainly be a pleasure to have a man as handsome as you at the helm of the Honeymoon Hotel. You remind me of my dear Louie when we first met."

"When was that?" Richard asked politely.

"In 1946—right after the war. Oh, he was a handsome devil. Jet black hair, gleaming brown eyes, a noble chin—just like you, Mr. Chandler. He wasn't as tall or as broad across the chest, of course, but you remind me of him just the same."

Mrs. Delacroix placed her glasses on her nose, tilted back her head and peered at Richard through the half lenses. "It's not only how you look that reminds me of Louie, either. There's something else about you—an inner spark or fire or some such."

Passion, Kate silently agreed. Richard was completely, fervently absorbed in whatever he was doing at any given moment. She could only imagine what it be like to kiss a man who gave himself so intensely to whatever experience was at hand.

The thought sent a shiver chasing through her, and she rubbed her hands along the sleeves of her navy blazer. *That's something you'll never find out,* she scolded herself. In addition to all the other reasons he would be completely unsuitable as a romantic partner, Richard was her boss. That alone should be enough to place him completely off-limits. She needed to put this silly crush behind her and focus on her work, Kate reprimanded herself.

She deliberately directed her gaze back to Mrs. Delacroix, whose eyes had taken on a melancholy, nostalgic expression. The dear old soul looked as if she needed to talk, Kate thought, her heart turning over as it always did whenever she saw a person in need. She knew Richard was chomping at the bit to close this deal, but she couldn't resist the urge to boost the old woman's spirits. Kate believed in never passing up the chance to help someone feel better.

Besides, it wouldn't hurt Richard to wait a few more moments. And from what she'd seen of his revolving-door love life, it wouldn't hurt him to hear a tale of true love, either.

"How did you meet your husband?" Kate asked.

"At a masked ball during Mardi Gras." A dreamy expression softened the old woman's features. "I was disguised as

Cleopatra, and he'd come as Mark Anthony. At the time, he said it was fate. I later learned he'd seen me on the street and followed me to my dressmaker's shop. When he discovered I was being fitted for a costume ball, he slipped my seamstress a twenty to tell him what party I was going to and to describe my costume so he could dress accordingly.''

''How romantic,'' Kate breathed.

''Oh, it was. Louie just swept me off my feet. He was the most romantic man in the world. Why, he built this hotel to look just like the place where we stayed on our own honeymoon in Paris.''

''That's the lovliest thing I've ever heard,'' Kate said softly.

''Louie always said that if we could help love flourish, we'd be doing a great service to the world. He believed that the first few weeks of marriage set the tone for the rest of a couple's life together. So we dedicated our lives to giving newlyweds a wonderful start. We succeeded pretty well, too, based on the number of couples who return to celebrate their anniversaries here.'' Her soft smile faded into a long sigh. ''I've been running the place all by myself since Louie passed away two years ago, but my doctor says I need to start taking it easy. Seems I've developed a little heart trouble.''

''I'm so sorry,'' Kate murmured.

''Oh, I'll be fine. I just need to find a suitable buyer for this place and get into a less strenuous line of work.'' She gazed at Richard with regret. ''You're such a charming man, and you look so much like my Louie. It's a terrible shame I won't be able to sell the hotel to you.''

Richard gripped the arm of the love seat so tightly he nearly snapped off the head of the carved swan that adorned it. ''What do you mean, you can't sell it to me?''

He'd carefully researched the financial situations of both the hotel and its owner, and he knew Mrs. Delacroix needed to sell it badly—and not just on account of her health. The occupancy rate had steadily plummeted over the past few years, and now the hotel wasn't even taking in enough money to cover payroll expenses. Mrs. Delacroix was personally well-off, but she couldn't keep digging into her pockets indefinitely to pay her staff. She would have to sell the hotel soon.

And when she did, Richard intended to be the buyer. He'd wanted to own a hotel ever since childhood. This one would not only satisfy that craving but turn an enormous profit as well.

It was the find of a lifetime, a real plum. Located on the edge of the French Quarter, the six-story hotel had one hundred and twenty rooms, a large ballroom, a restaurant and a pool. Best of all, it was within easy walking distance of the convention center, and it had the potential to host small conferences itself. Once he'd completely gutted and overhauled the interior, positioned it as a business hotel and operated it long enough to prove its profitability, he could sell it for a fortune. And getting it in shape to resell should satisfy his lifelong urge to play hotelier.

But it wouldn't do to act overeager. It was always a mistake to give away how badly he wanted something. His personal rule of thumb was that his air of nonchalance should be directly proportional to how important an issue really was to him.

He forced his facial muscles to relax. "Was something in my proposal out of order?"

"Not in your proposal. In your résumé."

"My résumé?" Richard couldn't keep the note of incredulity out of his voice. He'd included his résumé to reassure Mrs. Delacroix that he was more than qualified to buy and operate her property. He mentally reviewed its contents—an MBA with honors from Tulane University, six promotions in two years at a commercial real-estate management firm, president and CEO of his own company at the age of twenty-eight, a millionaire at the age of twenty-nine. Now, at thirty-three, his financial statement was as solid as his credentials—especially since he'd just sold a small office building, a local dry-cleaning chain and a suburban strip mall in order to purchase the hotel.

How could she possibly find fault with his résumé?

"I've got it right here." The elderly woman perched her reading glasses back on her nose, picked up a folder and plucked out a piece of paper. Rapidly scanning it with her birdlike eyes, she tapped the bottom of the page with a bright pink fingernail. "Marital status—single."

"So?"

"So, you're not married."

The old broad was as nutty as a French Market pecan praline, Richard thought darkly. "I don't see how that could pose a problem."

Mrs. Delacroix put down the paper and somberly gazed at him over the rim of her glasses. "Oh, but it does. I promised my dear Louie I would only sell our hotel to a nice married couple as deeply in love with each other as we were."

"I fail to see what my marital status has to do with my qualifications," Richard sputtered.

"Quite a lot, I'm afraid." Mrs. Delacroix leaned forward, her round face earnest. "You'll probably think I'm a hopeless romantic, Mr. Chandler, but Louie and I always believed that only a happily married couple could fill this place with the warmth and love our guests deserve."

Richard's mouth fell open. He abruptly closed it and struggled to maintain his composure, his thoughts spinning.

The old woman lived in the hotel, and although she planned to move out when the property was sold, she considered it her home as well as her business. His real-estate appraiser had warned him that Mrs. Delacroix was sentimentally attached to the property and might be reluctant to sell if she knew of his plans to change and resell it.

As a precaution, Richard had kept his renovation scheme completely secret. Even Kate, who usually knew the details of all his dealings, thought he'd liquidated most of his assets because he intended to focus his energies on operating the hotel. What Kate didn't know wouldn't hurt her, he'd decided.

But what Richard didn't know himself was another story. No one had mentioned a word about matrimony being a condition of sale, and at the moment, he didn't have a clue how to deal with such a bizarre turn of events.

Richard's gaze involuntarily shifted to Kate. She had what he considered terrific interpersonal skills—a warm, empathetic personality that drew people out, opened them up and made them want to agree with her. More than once, a simple comment from her had facilitated negotiations that had seemed in danger of breaking down.

But judging from the rhapsodic look on her face, no help would be forthcoming today. She looked completely captivated by the old biddy's romantic drivel, Richard observed glumly. Her hands were clasped to her chest and her eyes held such an enthralled expression that Richard was momentarily distracted from the problem at hand.

His gaze inadvertently slid down to her Cupid's-bow mouth. He'd never noticed before that Kate had such kissable lips. Richard yanked his eyes away and rubbed his jaw, trying to obliterate the troublesome thoughts. Kate was his secretary, for heaven's sake—the best one he'd ever had. Women came and went, but a secretary like Kate was a rare find.

Besides, this was neither the time nor the place to be thinking about anything other than a way of convincing this batty old dame to sell him the hotel. He wanted the place so badly he could taste it, and he prided himself on winning what he wanted.

Winning—it was what he lived for. Coming out on top was the sole thing in life that counted, and he felt fully alive only when he was pursuing a goal.

Problem was, as soon as he obtained one objective, he promptly lost interest in it and began looking for another. That was how he dealt with business. It was how he dealt with women. It was how he dealt with life. And more and more often lately, it left him feeling empty and restless.

Even more troublesome was the fact that it was becoming harder and harder to find anything he really wanted.

A cold, empty ache gnawed at his belly. He restlessly

shifted on the love seat, trying to thrust the disturbing thought from his mind.

Well, he wanted this hotel, he thought stubbornly—more than he'd ever wanted anything in his life. He'd sold off most of his other holdings in order to purchase it, and he was determined to do so.

He turned his most engaging smile on Mrs. Delacroix. "I'm sure there's a way we can work together on this," he cajoled.

The matron shook her head, making the flesh under her chin wobble like a turkey's wattle. "I'm afraid not, Mr. Chandler. Not unless you're planning to marry soon."

"Well, who says I'm not?" The rejoinder slipped out without warning, startling Richard as much as Mrs. Delacroix.

The elderly woman smiled so widely that the crow's feet around her eyes nearly cawed. "Oh, my! Well, this certainly puts the situation in a whole new light." She wagged a playful finger at him. "Why on earth didn't you tell me you were engaged?"

"I—uh, didn't think of it," Richard said hesitantly, wondering what he'd just let himself in for. He'd made the remark facetiously, but Mrs. Delacroix evidently wasn't taking it that way.

The deception nagged at his conscience, but his business sense told him the remark had probably salvaged his chance of getting the hotel.

"So who's the lucky lady?"

"Lucky lady?" Richard echoed blankly, thinking fast. He hadn't been seriously involved with anyone in months. People probably assumed he was bedding the steady stream of attractive post-debs he routinely escorted to New Orleans's social events, but the same restless apathy that had plagued his business life lately was afflicting his romantic life as well.

It was always the same old hassle, he thought grimly, even though he made a point of telling every woman he ever got involved with that he had no intention of getting married. For some unknown reason, each one thought she'd be the woman to change his mind.

It even followed a predictable pattern. A few months into a relationship, the lady-of-the-moment would make a declaration of love. When Richard didn't respond in kind, a big, tearful scene would follow. He always wound up feeling like a heel, even though he'd been completely up-front from the beginning.

Why couldn't women just take a man at his word? he wondered. Everything he'd ever seen or experienced had convinced him that what women called love was nothing more than the first stages of lust. All relationships eventually cooled down and ended—and if a man had been besotted enough to marry in the heat of passion, he usually got the short end of the stick in divorce court.

Why couldn't women just acknowledge they were sharing a temporary, mutually satisfying, physical relationship and leave it at that? Why did they always have to delude themselves into thinking it was something more? Why did they have to make something so basic and simple so emotionally complex?

Lately it all just seemed like too much of an effort.

He exhaled a harsh breath, then realized Mrs. Delacroix was looking at him expectantly. He needed to come up with a fiancée, and he needed to do it fast.

He glanced again at Kate. She was staring at him wide-eyed, her mouth open, her green eyes round and confused.

Inspiration struck. He reached out and grabbed her hand. "It's, uh, Kate, here. She's just about the luckiest lady I know."

Richard heard Kate's sharp intake of breath. He forced a smile as she stared at him blankly, her face two shades paler than normal, her lips parted in an openmouthed gape. She seemed to be carved out of ice. He gave her hand a hard squeeze, hoping to jolt her out of it.

Mrs. Delacroix cackled with amusement. "Why, Kate—you sly thing! Sitting there so primly, acting as if you were just his secretary!"

Her pale face suddenly flushed bright red. "But—but—I'm actually…" she mumbled.

Richard broke in. "Sweetheart, there's no reason to continue pretending now that Mrs. Delacroix knows all about us." He patted her hand and turned back to the old lady. "Kate thinks it's unprofessional to tell people we're engaged."

"Why, I think it's wonderful! Do you intend to work together after you're married?"

"Kate and I plan to continue working together for the foreseeable future." That much, at least, was the truth, Richard thought—if Kate didn't quit in anger the moment they left here. He glanced at her, trying to gauge her reaction. She still seemed to be in a state of shock.

"Louie and I always worked together," Mrs. Delacroix said approvingly. "I think it's one of the reasons we had such a close marriage. In fact, his office connects to this one." The elderly woman looked from Richard to Kate. "So when's the wedding? You must tell me all about your plans, Kate dear."

Kate gazed at Richard, her eyes filled with panic.

"We—er—haven't had time to make them yet," Richard said rapidly. "This is a rather recent turn of events."

"I see." Mrs. Delacroix looked rapidly from one to the other, her eyes so bright and shrewd that Richard feared she saw right through him. "Well, as soon as you're properly married, I'll be happy to reopen our discussion."

Richard shifted uneasily. "There's no reason we can't go ahead and settle things now."

"Oh?" Mrs. Delacroix arched one of the painted slashes on her forehead that passed for eyebrows. "Do you plan to marry soon, then?"

Richard nodded.

Mrs. Delacroix's eyes narrowed in what Richard feared was an expression of suspicion. "Kate, my dear, I haven't heard you say a word. What kind of wedding do you have in mind?"

Richard swallowed hard and gazed at Kate, silently pleading for help. She was a paragon of helpfulness; she took his Mercedes through a car wash every time she used it to run an errand for him; she remembered the birthdays of everyone in the office and sent cards to them in his name; and she often gave up her holidays and evenings to help him catch up on paperwork. When he'd had the flu last month, she'd even brought homemade chicken soup to his Garden District home. But for all of her helpfulness, Kate had a definite mind of her own, and Richard wasn't at all sure how she would take to posing as his fiancée.

There was a lot about Kate he didn't know, he suddenly realized—including whether or not she had a boyfriend who might seriously object to this scheme. He deliberately kept from learning too much about his employees' personal lives in order to keep his distance.

His stomach knotted with uncertainty as he watched Kate turn to Mrs. Delacroix.

"I, uh, really haven't had time to think about it." Her voice sounded slightly hoarse. "As Richard said—this is all pretty sudden."

Richard realized he'd been holding his breath. He pressed her hand in gratitude.

"Surely you have some idea what kind of wedding you want," Mrs. Delacroix persisted. "Most women have been dreaming about it since they were little girls."

Kate glanced at Richard again. He gave an encouraging nod and squeezed her fingers, which felt as cold and stiff as icicles in his hand. "Go ahead and tell her—*darling.*"

Kate's cheeks flamed at the endearment. She drew a deep, shaky breath. "Well… I—I want an evening wedding. Something small and simple—no bridesmaids, just my best friend, Annie, as my maid of honor. And a white dress, of course— with a train, and maybe some beadwork on the bodice. And a veil—preferably fingertip length—with pearls sprinkled all over it. And candlelight. And violins. And I've always dreamed of carrying a bouquet of magnolias and white roses."

Richard stared at her in surprise. Either Kate was a better actress than he'd ever imagined or else she'd given this issue a lot of thought. Maybe she was even engaged to someone and actually planning a wedding, he thought with alarm.

"Sounds lovely." Mrs. Delacroix nodded approvingly. "Richard said you planned to marry soon. How soon?"

"I—uh, don't..."

"As soon as possible," Richard interjected. "This weekend, if I can talk Kate into it."

Mrs. Delacroix leaned back and chortled. "That's what I like to see—an eager bridegroom! Well, I never believed in long engagements, either. My Louie and I married just six weeks after we met." She gave a contented sigh and folded her plump hands on her desk. "Where do you intend to have it?"

"We, uh, aren't sure."

"Well, you must invite me. If I'm going to sell you my hotel, I'd love to see you launch your new life together."

If I'm going to sell you my hotel. The words sent a rush of adrenaline pounding through Richard's veins—the same rush he always felt when victory was within his grasp. Her ridiculous terms of sale suddenly seemed insignificant in light of the fact the hotel might soon be his. "So you'll consider my buyout proposal?" he asked, leaning forward.

Mrs. Delacroix smiled. "I'll do better than that. As soon as you're married, I'll accept it. Conditionally, of course."

The sense of triumph froze in his chest. "What do you mean, conditionally?"

The old woman twirled the enormous diamond wedding set on her left hand. "I promised my Louie that before I sold the hotel, I'd have the buyer operate it for a trial period. You see, many of our guests are returning to celebrate their anniversaries, and they expect to have the same wonderful service they experienced on their first visit. So after you marry, I'd like for you to manage the hotel for a month. Then, if everything goes well—and I'm sure that it will—why, then we'll sign the final papers."

A wedding, a month-long trial... Richard frowned. What

would this ditzy old dame want next? A séance with her dear
departed Louie?

This was getting completely out of hand, Richard thought
grimly. Maybe he should back off and let Mrs. Delacroix think
he was losing interest. "I'll have to consult with my attorneys
and get back with you."

"Fine, but you'd better hurry. I've got two other offers, and
I intend to make a decision soon." Her brightly painted lips
curved up in a smile. "I would dearly love to sell the hotel
to *you*, though, Mr. Chandler. You're so much like my Louie.
And I adore the idea of newlyweds running the place."

Two other offers! Richard's jaw tensed. He'd heard a rumor
that a major hotel chain was interested in buying the property.
If another company was vying for it as well, the bidding would
rapidly escalate beyond his reach. His current offer was
stretching all of his resources as it was.

The thought of someone else buying the hotel out from under him set his teeth on edge. Winning was important, but not
losing was essential.

He wouldn't blow this deal over a couple of inconsequential
requests, he decided suddenly. He could handle anything for
a month—including a phony marriage.

Time enough later to work out the details. Right now, he
just needed to lock up the sale.

He pasted on what he hoped was a convincing smile. "Let's
forget about the lawyers, then. As far as I'm concerned, you've
got a deal."

"Wonderful!" Mrs. Delacroix clapped her hands together.
"But the first order of business is to get you two married."
Her smile suddenly widened. "I have a marvelous idea! You
can have the wedding here, in the hotel ballroom. We'll sched-
ule it for next Saturday. We can set up some flowered arches,
fill the room with candles, hire a string quartet. How does that
sound?"

About as pleasant as an unsedated tooth extraction, Richard
thought grimly. He managed a tight smile. "Kate and I will
have to talk it over."

"The kind of wedding Kate described will be next to impossible to pull together in less than a week. You'll need some help. If you hold it here, I can organize it for you. What place could be more perfect than the hotel you'll soon be operating together?"

Holy Toledo. He wasn't just in over his head—he was six feet under and covered with dirt. A heavy, sinking feeling settled in Richard's stomach like a boulder.

Mrs. Delacroix's bright blue eyes twinkled with excitement. "Just because you want to get married quickly doesn't mean Kate should be shortchanged on her dreams. You only get married once, you know."

Less than that, if I have anything to say about it.

"Oh, I can't wait. It'll be just perfect! We'll drape the room in white tulle and dim all the chandeliers...."

Richard suddenly felt as if he were suffocating, as if the pink walls were closing in and crushing him. He needed to get out of here, and quick. He grabbed Kate by the arm and hauled her to her feet. "That's, uh, very generous of you. We'll talk more about it tomorrow. Now, if you'll excuse us, we really need to get back to the office. I'm running late for a meeting."

"I'll go ahead and start making arrangements," Mrs. Delacroix called after him as he steered Kate to the door. "We've got a lot to do. Weddings don't just spontaneously happen, you know."

Could have fooled me. His mouth set in a tight line, Richard hustled Kate through the office door—a door he'd entered thirty minutes earlier, never dreaming that the next time he crossed its threshold, he'd be engaged to be married.

Chapter Two

Kate managed to hold her tongue until they'd stepped out the heavy brass doors of the hotel's side entrance and into the even heavier French Quarter air. By biting her lip, she even managed to wait until the valet had brought around Richard's red Mercedes sports coupe and they'd both climbed inside.

But the moment Richard started steering the car onto Decatur Street, she let him have it. "Are you out of your mind?" she demanded. "That sweet old lady's in there planning a wedding!"

Richard's expression was maddeningly calm. "Sure seems like it," he agreed.

"So what on earth are you going to do about it?"

"Hmm." Richard rubbed his chin as if he were deeply pondering the question. "Well, I guess I'll just have to marry you."

"Excuse me?"

She didn't think she could possibly feel more shocked, but she bumped against Richard's shoulder as he suddenly swerved to miss a horse-drawn carriage. A rush of heat shot down her arm, despite the chill in the damp March air. She drew back and tightened her seat belt, hating the way her heart pounded at his touch, hating the way she suddenly felt disoriented and rattled and confused.

Well, no wonder she felt that way, she thought, trying to calm her runaway emotions. He'd just announced in a matter-of-fact tone that he intended to marry her, as if he were telling her to take a memo. It was enough to disconcert anyone.

Especially someone who'd been secretly fantasizing about him for months.

She lifted her chin and hid her pounding heart under a show of bravado. "I don't believe my job description mentions anything about marriage."

"You must not have read the fine print."

"Very funny." Kate stared out the window, appalled that he could joke about such a serious matter.

Richard reached over and patted her hand. "Relax. We'll *get* married, but we won't really *be* married. We'll go through with a ceremony for Mrs. Delacroix's benefit, but we'll skip all the legal requirements."

She knew he hadn't been sincere about marrying her, of course, but hearing him speak of it so dismissively rankled all the same. "You're taking an awful lot for granted, aren't you? What makes you think I'll go along with a crazy scheme like this?"

That irritating smile was still plastered on his face. "Probably the fact that you already have."

Kate gazed blankly out the windshield, chafing at the thought of how she'd helped him mislead the poor old woman. "That's only because you put me on the spot. What was I supposed to do—hang you out to dry?"

He braked for a red light at the Canal Street intersection, then turned toward her, all traces of amusement gone. "You'd have been well within your rights if you had. I had no business putting you in an awkward situation like that. Thanks for bailing me out."

His eyes were as warm and dark as a double espresso, and the effect they had on her was just as strong and stimulating.

It was impossible to feel angry when he looked at her like that. It was almost impossible to think. Flustered, she glanced away and tried to muster a modicum of her former indignation. "The whole idea is ridiculous anyway. It would never work."

"Sure it would. We'd have to act all lovey-dovey when she's around, but it would be a small price to pay for getting a hotel in this location." He flashed a killer grin. "And I'll make sure you're well compensated for your trouble."

Kate didn't know what galled her more—the thought of deceiving the kindly old lady, the offer of money to do it or the inference that acting affectionately toward her would be a chore. "I don't want any part of it," she stated flatly, averting her eyes from his distractingly handsome face. Whenever she looked at him, the pull of attraction weakened all of her resolve. "Mrs. Delacroix loves that hotel. Besides, she made a solemn promise to her dead husband."

"We'd be doing her a favor."

The seriousness of his tone made her venture another glance at him, although she knew it was dangerous for her to do so. "What do you mean?"

"I've heard rumors that Consolidated Hotels is interested in buying it, and they don't even operate any hotels with less than five hundred rooms. If they get their hands on it, they'll knock the place down and build a one thousand-room skyscraper like the Marriott or Sheraton."

The front of the hotel was visible from the intersection. Kate studied it through her side window, taking in the handsome marble stairs, the enormous brass doors, the row of carved cherubs frolicking on the stonework above the first floor. The idea of a wrecking ball smashing into it appalled her. "But it's so quaint—so charming!"

Richard rested his arm on the steering wheel and leaned forward to view the building. "I happen to think it's pretty special myself—with the exception of Mrs. Delacroix's office."

Kate couldn't help but smile at the reference to the ghastly decor.

"I think the hotel's just the right size, too," Richard continued. "Unlike the folks at Consolidated, I wouldn't want the overhead of a larger place. But the land it's on is worth more than the building." The light changed, and Richard turned his attention back to the intersection.

Kate continued to gaze at the impressive building until it was out of sight. "Aren't there historic-preservation laws that prevent skyscrapers from going up in the French Quarter?"

"They don't apply to property that fronts Canal Street. The Honeymoon Hotel misses the historic district by exactly a block."

"But surely Mrs. Delacroix wouldn't sell it to someone who plans to tear it down!"

"Not knowingly. But a company like Consolidated will tell her anything she wants to hear."

"Oh, I see. Unlike anything you'd ever do, right?" Kate said dryly.

She was gratified that Richard had the grace to look sheepish. "Hey, I never exactly told her we were engaged. She just jumped to that conclusion."

Kate viewed him through narrowed eyes. "She didn't jump. She was pushed."

Richard laughed, his eyes crinkling in a way that made Kate's pulse accelerate. "However she arrived at it, the fact remains that she needs to sell her hotel. If it's easier for her to part with it if she thinks we're married, where's the harm? Especially when you consider the alternative. If I don't buy it, she'll end up selling it to what she thinks is a nice mom-and-pop couple, only to discover afterward that they were a just front for Consolidated."

When he put it that way, it sounded as if he were doing Mrs. Delacroix a kindness. And he very well might be, Kate admitted. She'd seen the kind of hardball some of Richard's competitors could play; double-dealing and deception were just part of a day's work. Richard might be work-obsessed, overly competitive and sadly misguided about love and marriage, but he had a strong streak of basic decency, and he'd always been straightforward in his business dealings.

She'd never seen him as deadset on a project as he was on this one, though. She glanced up at him curiously as they waited for a light to change. "This project seems awfully important to you."

"It is."

"Why?"

He lifted his wide shoulders. "Sentimental reasons, I guess. I've always wanted to own a hotel. My favorite memories from childhood are of a hotel my uncle operated."

She'd never heard Richard say anything about his childhood—or his sentiments, either, for that matter. She was dying to know what made him tick. Maybe if she could figure him out, she could get over her strange fascination with him. "Did your parents take you there for vacations?"

Richard gave a dry laugh. "Hardly. You might say I went there to vacation *from* my parents."

"What do you mean?"

He guided the car onto Poydras Street. "Before their divorce, my parents were always fighting. Uncle Joe's hotel was just a few blocks from our town house in Dallas, so I used to go there to get away from all the screaming and yelling."

Images of Kate's own parents flitted through her mind—her mother gazing adoringly across the dinner table at her father, her dad winking conspiratorially as he sneaked up to surprise her mom with a kiss, the frequent hugs, the smiles, the easy laughter. Her parents' affection for each other had been the foundation of Kate's family. They hadn't had much in the way of money, but their home had been rich in love. How awful, Kate thought, to have grown up in a house filled instead with anger and turmoil. The information went a long ways toward explaining his attitude about marriage.

"That must have been very difficult," she said softly.

"It wasn't much fun," he admitted.

"Were things better after the divorce?"

"Depends on your definition of better. There was no fighting, but in some ways the silence was worse."

Compassion flooded Kate's heart. "Did you live with your mom or your dad?"

Richard pulled a hand from the steering wheel and raked it through his thick hair. "I ping-ponged back and forth until they finally sent me off to boarding school. They shared joint custody, but the real custodians were a long string of nannies." The corners of his mouth tugged into a wry grin. "I was what's commonly called a difficult child. The longest a nanny ever stayed on the job was six months."

"Why?"

His mouth quirked into a grin. "Gee, I don't know. Maybe it had something to do with the earthworms I'd put in their handbags or the mice I'd hide in their beds or the stink bombs that would find their way into their face cream."

Kate laughed even though his tale had touched a soft spot in her heart. "How did your parents handle your behavior?"

Richard gave a careless shrug, but the tense lines around his mouth told Kate she'd hit a nerve. "Ignored me, mostly. Dad was busy with his ever-expanding law practice, and Mom was preoccupied with her social life and beauty treatments. The only time they paid any attention to me was when a nanny gave notice and I interfered with their schedules."

Kate gazed at his handsome profile, her heart aching at the thought of the lonely little boy trying to get his parents' attention the only way he knew how. She could tell by the rigid set of his jaw that the memory still hurt.

"But none of that matters now," he said, changing the subject as deftly as he changed traffic lanes. "What matters now is whether or not you'll help me get the Honeymoon Hotel."

She'd learned more about him in the past five minutes than she'd learned in the entire preceding eight months. It might be another eight months before he was willing to open up again. If she was ever going to figure him out, she needed to keep him talking now. "Is Mrs. Delacroix's place much like your uncle's?"

He seemed to consider the question as he slowed for a jay-walker. "Quite a bit. Both hotels were built in the late forties, and they're about the same size. Uncle Joe's place was a little smaller, but it was a class act all the way—a real little jewel." His eyes took on a faraway look. "It was always filled with fresh flowers. One of the things I remember most was the way it smelled like flowers. I remember the way the lobby sounded, too—full of tinkling glass and music and laughter."

"Sounds like you've got fond memories."

"Oh, I do. Uncle Joe was the greatest. Whenever I showed up, he always acted like he was really glad to see me, like he desperately needed my help. He'd put me right to work—bussing tables or cleaning rooms or washing dishes or what-ever needed to be done. I loved working there. It made me feel like…" He lifted his shoulders in a shrug, evidently trying to downplay the importance of what he was about to say. "…like I belonged or something."

Was that why Richard was so obsessed with work now, Kate wondered—because it made him feel like he belonged? She'd always sensed a loneliness about him, an aloofness that had nothing to do with coldness or unfriendliness. He'd always seemed somehow isolated, as if he was unable to connect to people on anything but a superficial level.

No wonder he was so intent on buying a hotel, she thought suddenly. It was the one place where he'd felt really welcome, really wanted. The knowledge cracked a chink in the protec-tive armor she'd built around her heart, allowing an unau-thorized sensation of warmth and tenderness toward him to seep in.

"Does your uncle still have the hotel?" she asked softly.

Richard shook his head. "He sold it while I was in college, then he died a short while later. Now it's nothing but a run-down old apartment building. I looked into buying it, but the neighborhood has deteriorated, and there's no market for a hotel in that location anymore." He shifted restlessly on the seat, then glanced at Kate. She could almost feel him trying to shake off the memories. "In that respect, it's completely unlike Mrs. Delacroix's property. Her hotel has become more valuable over time, and it'll continue to appreciate.''

He turned the car into the parking garage of their office building on St. Charles Avenue, stopping to insert his plastic card in the machine at the gate. When the red-and-white-striped bar lifted, he steered his Mercedes up the ramp and into the darkened garage. The subdued lighting matched his expression as he pulled into his personalized parking spot.

He killed the engine and turned toward her, his eyes dark and intent. ''This is the most important deal of my life, Kate—so important that I'm putting all my assets on the line to buy this place. But I can't do it without your help.''

The dim artificial light of the garage cast shadows on his face, accentuating his strong cheekbones, the plane of his jaw, the deep cleft in his chin. His eyes were dark and searching, and Kate's stomach quivered when they locked on hers. ''I know it's asking a lot, but we'd only have to pretend to be married for a month. What do you say? Will you help me out?''

She'd always had trouble refusing a direct plea for help—had always been an easy mark for telephone solicitors and street beggars, a soft touch for needy friends and acquaintances. So how could she refuse to help Richard now, especially when she'd just discovered the heart-wrenching reason he wanted the hotel?

Her head warned her she was making a drastic mistake, but her heart gave her no other option. The heat of his imploring gaze melted the last shred of her already weakened resistance.

Swallowing hard, she slowly nodded.

''Attagirl!'' Richard's smile seemed to light up the dim interior of the car. Kate's heart thudded as he bounded out of the car, circled it and opened her door. The next thing she knew, he'd pulled her to her feet and lifted her off the ground.

''You're the best, Kate!''

She was unprepared for the feel of his solid chest against her breasts, his hard thighs against her legs, his muscular arms around her back as he jubilantly swung her around...unprepared to find her nose against his neck, to discover herself inhaling the shockingly erotic scent of his shampoo and shaving cream. The sudden onslaught of sensations left her giddy and dizzy and more than a little light-headed.

By the time he set her back on the ground, her pulse was roaring in her ears. He drew back and gazed at her, and the look in his eyes stole the breath from her lungs. His expression had changed from jubilation to something else—something smoky and warm, something that thickened the air and heated her blood and made it hard for her to breathe.

Arousal. Oh, dear heaven, was he feeling it, too?

His arms were still around her, his hands on her back, and his fingers seemed to burn through her wool blazer. The moment had long since passed when someone should have moved, someone should have spoken.

Kate couldn't have done either, even if she'd been so inclined. All she could do was stare at him, mesmerized, unable to breathe, or to move, or to think of anything except the thrilling, terrifying certainty that she was about to be kissed. His face was drawing closer, and his eyes had an intent, heavy-lidded expression that made her heart flutter like a captured bird.

A loud, sudden honk made them both jump. Kate jerked her eyes toward the sound and saw a white sedan three feet away, the driver impatiently gesturing them out of the vacant parking spot where they were standing.

Richard tugged her arm and pulled her aside. Kate wobbled on her low-heeled pumps, her knees the consistency of the gumbo she'd had for lunch.

Oh, mercy. She'd thought getting some personal insight into what made him tick would help her handle the insane attraction she felt for him, but it seemed to have had just the opposite effect.

Richard dropped her arm and stepped back as the car pulled into the slot. Kate stood perfectly still, rooted to the spot, as the driver slammed his door, eyed them curiously and headed for the building.

Richard cleared his throat and thrust his hands in his pockets. "I really appreciate your help, Kate."

Act normal, she ordered herself, pulling her jacket around her like a shield. After all, Richard looked as if nothing at all had happened.

But then, nothing had—had it? He'd picked her up and swung her around in an innocent, spontaneous gesture of celebration. Nothing had really transpired between them—nothing that she could put her finger on, anyway. That she felt fogheaded and rubber-legged and more than a little disappointed was probably due to the dim lighting and her own overactive imagination.

She tried to smile, but her lips felt too stiff to cooperate. "I just hope we can pull it off. I don't know a whole lot about acting—" what was that phrase he'd used? "—lovey-dovey."

Oh, dear—she sounded like a neophyte schoolgirl. "In public, I mean."

Oh, no—what would he think she did in private? Her cheeks burned as she scrambled to correct any misguided impressions she might have created. "I mean, I've only been in one long-term relationship, and he wasn't—I mean, we weren't—very openly affectionate. I'm afraid I might not be a very lovey-dovey person."

Any more lovey-dovey and he'd need a cold shower, Richard thought darkly, ramming his fingers through his hair. He hadn't anticipated how holding Kate would affect him—how sweet her slight weight would feel in his arms, how warm her small breasts would feel against his chest, how downy soft her cheek would feel on his neck. He'd been completely unprepared for the breath-sucking, mind-numbing, sock-scorching impact of her body against his. He couldn't remember ever getting so unexpectedly arousal in his life.

He shifted his feet and buttoned the jacket of his charcoal business suit to hide the evidence. Holy cow, if that car hadn't come along when it had, he'd have lost all control and kissed her.

What in blazes had gotten into him? He'd never thought

about Kate in these terms before. She was entirely too strait-laced and conservative for his tastes. He was used to women who dressed to flaunt their figures, and Kate dressed to blend in to the woodwork. Why, he'd seen her on a daily basis for the past eight months, and he still had no idea what her body looked like under those drab, shapeless jackets she always wore. The darn things covered her like a suit of armor.

With a start, he realized he was scowling down at her. A stab of guilt shot through him at the worried expression on her upturned face.

Hell's bells, it wasn't her fault. He'd had no business grabbing her like that, much less responding to her like a randy bull. Besides, from the comments she'd just made, it sounded as though she had pretty limited experience with men.

He searched for a way to reassure her. "It's easy. All you have to do is follow my lead and pretend you're sexually attracted to me."

Her face flushed scarlet, a fact that struck Richard as nothing short of amazing. Kate was usually as self-possessed as she was kindhearted.

Was she attracted to him? He'd never considered the possibility before.

He stared at her, searching for a clue. She exhibited none of the usual signs. She never flirted, she didn't dress provocatively and she didn't cast suggestive glances his way. As a matter of fact, he couldn't even imagine her doing any of those things. How the heck would a woman like Kate behave if she *were* attracted to a man?

Was she attracted to him? By golly, this could drive him crazy.

She lifted her chin to a combative angle under his scrutiny. "Married people aren't just attracted to each other. They're in love."

Richard forced himself to stop staring. "It's the same thing."

"It most certainly is not! Marriage is the closest bond two

people can share, and it involves emotions a whole lot stronger than attraction.''

There was nothing to be gained by arguing with her. He lifted his shoulders. ''Well, since neither of us knows what marriage really feels like, let's just pretend to have a big-time case of the hots for each other.''

He wouldn't have thought it was possible, but her face turned even redder.

Was she attracted to him? Nah. That was just wishful thinking.

Wishful thinking? Holy Moses, did he *want* her to be attracted to him?

Of course not, he assured himself. He was just a red-blooded male awash in hormones after an unexpectedly explosive physical encounter, that was all. The last thing he wanted was to get involved with his buttoned-down, marriage-enamored secretary.

But he *did* want her to pretend to marry him. And from the troubled expression in her moss green eyes, she looked as though she might back out at any moment.

''This whole thing will be a piece of cake,'' he reassured her.

''I'm not so sure. I'm a terrible liar.''

''You won't have to lie. I'll handle the explanations. The only thing you'll have to misrepresent will be our marital status.''

''Promise?''

''Promise.''

The tension in her face seemed to lessen, but he could tell she was unconvinced. He tried again. ''All we have to do is let Mrs. Delacroix see a wedding, then act like newlyweds whenever she's around. There's nothing to it.''

Yeah, right, his mind mocked. Based on his reaction to Kate today, the problem wouldn't be acting as if he were attracted to her when they were with Mrs. Delacroix; the problem would be acting as if he weren't when they were alone.

He hoped the smile he gave her was more convincing than it felt. ''It'll all be over in a month. How hard can it be?''

Chapter Three

Harder than he'd ever imagined, Richard thought the next morning. He'd no sooner gotten off the phone with Mrs. Delacroix, who'd called to say she was on her way over to discuss wedding plans, than Kate buzzed him on the intercom.

Richard leaned over his massive mahogany desk and pressed the button. "Yes?"

"The gossip columnist for *The Times-Picayune* is on line three. She wants to know if it's true that the most eligible bachelor in New Orleans is about to get married."

"How the heck did she find out about that?" Richard demanded.

"Apparently through an orchestra leader Mrs. Delacroix contacted."

Blast. He hadn't intended for everyone in New Orleans to know about this pseudo marriage. Now there was no chance of keeping it quiet.

"Tell her I'm tied up in a meeting and I'll get back to her. Then come on in here, Kate. We've got to formulate a game plan before Mrs. Delacroix arrives."

But before he could even press the disconnect button, a tall, angry blonde stormed through his office door. Startled, Richard rose from behind his desk as his former girlfriend advanced on him like Sherman on Atlanta. "Michelle—what a surprise."

To put it mildly. They hadn't spoken in four months—not since the ugly argument when she'd issued the "marry me or it's over between us" ultimatum.

"Don't Michelle me." She slammed her purse on his desk and leaned over it toward him, her carefully made-up blue eyes shooting pure venom. "It's true, isn't it? I can tell from that guilty look on your face."

"What's true?" he asked warily.

"That you're getting married."

Kate suddenly appeared in the doorway. "I'm sorry, but you can't just barge in on Mr. Chandler without an appointment," she said, her voice crisp and businesslike.

"Go tend to your filing and leave us alone," the blonde snarled. She whipped back toward Richard, leaned forward across the desk and bared her orthodontically perfect teeth. "When we broke up, you told me you weren't the marrying kind. I happen to know you've said the same thing to at least half a dozen other women since. So how come you're suddenly engaged? I demand to know what's going on."

Richard jammed his hands in his pockets with deliberate casualness. "Beats me. Guess I just got swept away."

He could tell from the feral curl of her lip that it wasn't the answer she wanted to hear. "Who is she?"

"No one you really know."

"I heard she's a nobody."

Offended by the snobbish remark, Richard reflexively glanced at Kate. Her face had grown so ashen that the faint freckles on her nose were visible clear across the room.

Something protective kicked into gear in the center of his chest. He gazed at Michelle's anger-twisted face, wondering what he'd ever seen in her. "Then you heard wrong." He motioned Kate into the room. "Kate, I'm sure you remember Michelle. Michelle, this is Kate—my fiancée."

Michelle stared at her as if she were a space alien. "Your secretary?" she gasped, saying the word with a degree of horror usually reserved for B-grade Halloween movies.

"My fiancée," he said firmly. He reached an arm around Kate. She stiffened noticeably at his touch. For some reason, her resistance made him pull her even closer.

"Well, well, well." Malevolence oozed from the catty blonde's voice. "Haven't you done well for yourself? I suppose congratulations are in order."

Richard noted that Michelle failed to extend them. Kate stiffened even further but managed to ignore the slight. "Thank you."

Michelle twisted her lips into an artificial smile. "I saw Richard at the Opera Ball just last weekend, and he was with a tall blonde. Exactly how long have you two been seeing each other?"

The inference that he'd been cheating on her with another woman was unmistakable. Kate shot him an alarmed look.

Richard squeezed her arm in encouragement. "That was a foolish effort on my part to make Kate jealous. I had a hard time convincing her to marry me. When she finally agreed last night, she made me the happiest man on earth." He smiled down at Kate in what he hoped was an adoring fashion, then turned back to Michelle. "How did you hear about our engagement?"

Displeasure distorted her face into a cold mask of fury. "From my florist. He's evidently providing the flowers for your—your—*ceremony*." She spat out the word as if it were a rotten oyster, evidently unable to bring herself to say *wedding*. "This Saturday at the Honeymoon Hotel, from what I understand. What an odd place to get married. And so soon! Why, it's almost enough to make a body wonder if there's some reason to rush." She gazed from Richard to Kate, arching one carefully tweezed eyebrow. "Is there?"

Kate's face flushed scarlet.

Oh, hell. Richard hadn't thought of this— that people would think he was marrying Kate so quickly because he'd gotten her in trouble. He scowled, hating the idea of making Kate an object of public speculation. This charade was filled with more unforeseen problems than a swim meet in an alligator swamp.

He swallowed back the caustic retort on the tip of his tongue and forced a smile. "The only reason we're rushing is because we just can't stand to wait." He cast his most adoring gaze at Kate and slid his hand from her arm to her waist. "Isn't that right, sweetheart?"

Kate's eyes widened, but she rose to the occasion with admirable aplomb. She placed a hand on his chest.

"That's right. We should invite your friend here to the wedding, don't you think, honey?"

Richard grinned down and Kate smiled up; when their eyes met, it felt as if they were the only two people in the room. The soft weight of her hand on his chest made his heart pound so hard he was certain she could feel it.

All this talk about marriage must have addled his brain. He'd nearly jumped Kate's bones yesterday in the garage, and here he was thinking along the same lines again this morning. What in blazes was the matter with him? This was Kate, for Pete's sake—good old, reliable, efficient, dependable Kate.

But something about touching her made him forget about reliability and efficiency. By golly, why hadn't he noticed before now exactly how lovely her face was? She had the cutest little button of a nose, and her eyes were the most fascinating shade of green. Her hair curled around her shoulders in reckless abandon, completely at odds with the rest of her overly prim appearance. Those curls were simply begging to be touched.

He was about to reach out his free hand to do just that when Michelle snatched her purse from his desk, jolting him out of his reverie. She shot them both a look full of daggers. "Don't bother sending an invitation. I've got plans for Saturday."

"Well, it was nice of you to stop by." Kate sounded as gracious as a Southern belle at a tea party. "Maybe the three of us can get together sometime."

Richard chuckled as Michelle huffed out the door, nearly

bumping into Mrs. Delacroix in the process. The elderly woman swept into the room, craning her neck curiously to eye Michelle's retreating back.

Richard pulled Kate closer to his side, rationalizing that he needed to put on a show of affection for the old dowager. That Kate felt so delicious under his hand was just a side benefit.

He splayed his fingers, feeling the indentation of her waist under her stern gray suit. He'd discovered yesterday that she had curves under all those bulky jackets, and those curves had been on his mind ever since.

Mrs. Delacroix smiled at them approvingly. "You two seem like a pair of happy lovebirds this morning." She nodded her head in the direction of Michelle's departure. "But the gal that just left here looked mad as a wet hen. What on earth is the matter with her, Kate, dear?"

Kate pulled away from Richard's embrace. Her cheeks were pinker than normal, her eyes looked strangely bright and her hand had a slight tremor as she reached up and smoothed her hair. Was she nervous about pretending to be engaged in front of Mrs. Delacroix? Richard wondered. Or was she as jolted by the unexpected electricity between them as he was?

Kate tugged at her jacket, straightening it at the exact spot his hand had just rested. "That was Richard's old girlfriend. She wasn't any too happy to learn he's getting married."

Mrs. Delacroix chuckled and lowered herself onto one of the upholstered chairs opposite Richard's desk, adjusting the yards of hot pink silk that made up today's outlandish ensemble. "Louie left a few gals wringing out their hankies when he married me, too. Well, you just never mind, dearie. It only means you've landed yourself a prize." She smiled at Kate and patted the chair beside her. "I bet you've left a broken heart or two out there yourself."

Richard's chest tightened with a baffling anxiety.

Kate glanced at him, then gave a vague smile. "Oh, I'm sure they'll manage to survive."

The thought of Kate juggling a whole herd of suitors made Richard decidedly uneasy. Sitting on the corner of his desk, he loosened his tie and gazed at her, bewildered at his reaction. Kate's personal life was none of his business. She was an employee, after all, and that put her completely off-limits.

He must be bothered by the fact that it had taken him eight months to realize she was so desirable, he decided. He usually wasn't such a slow study where women were concerned.

"Maybe we can introduce your old flames to Richard's at the wedding," Mrs. Delacroix said.

The remark jerked Richard off the edge of his desk. "We won't be inviting anyone's old flames. We want to keep it small."

"Just your immediate family?" Mrs. Delacroix asked.

Family. Now there was a potentially disastrous complication. Why the heck hadn't he thought of it? "No one from my family will be attending. We're not very close. And none of Kate's family will be able to make it, either."

"My goodness. How very unusual. Doesn't she have any family?"

Was that an edge of suspicion in the old gal's eyes? Richard swallowed hard, wondering how the deuce to answer. He knew nothing about Kate's family, and he'd promised her she wouldn't have to lie in order to help him out. If he told a whopper, it might come back to haunt him. "She, uh, well— the fact of the matter is…" He frantically searched his mind for a plausible explanation.

Kate reached out and patted his hand. "It's okay, honey. It no longer hurts to talk about it." She turned to Mrs. Delacroix. "I lost both my parents my freshman year in college."

Richard gazed at her in surprise, both at the information and that she'd rushed to his rescue. Was it true? Something in her eyes told him that it was.

"You poor dear!" Mrs. Delacroix's painted brows pulled together in sympathy. "Well, what about other relatives? Any brothers or sisters?"

"Just one brother. He and his wife are missionaries in Kenya. There's no way they could make it back for the ceremony."

Mrs. Delacroix clucked sympathetically. "Well, don't you worry. You'll soon have all of the employees at the hotel as your family. That's how Louie and I always treated them, and I'm sure you'll do the same. In fact, I can't think of a better way to start things off than to invite them all to your wedding."

Richard's stomach squeezed into a hard knot. Holy Toledo. The quiet ceremony he'd envisioned had just grown into a three-ring circus. He thought fast, searching for a way to salvage the situation. "This is Kate's special day, and she's always dreamed of an intimate ceremony. Isn't that right, darling?"

Mrs. Delacroix sucked in her apple-shaped cheeks. "But the employees will be devastated if they're left out." She turned to Kate, her false-eyelash-fringed eyes round with concern. "You wouldn't want to hurt their feelings, would you, dear?"

Kate twisted her fingers in her lap. "Oh, no, I'd never deliberately hurt anyone's feelings, but..."

"See? And I know from your financial statement that cost isn't an issue—you can afford to make everyone happy, Mr. Chandler. Or may I call you Richard?"

"Please do," he said absently, his thoughts scurrying madly for a way out of this predicament.

"And you can call me Birdie."

"Birdie?"

"It's a nickname Louie gave me. He said my eyes were as blue as a parrot's wings."

"How sweet," Kate murmured.

"How...appropriate," Richard managed. Her husband had probably coined the nickname because he longed to put her in a draped cage, he thought darkly.

Mrs. Delacroix folded her hands together. "Well, then, it's settled. I have one hundred and fifty employees, and I'm sure you'll want to invite all your co-workers and business associates and friends. We'll plan on about three hundred people."

Three hundred people? "Now, look here, Mrs. Delacroix—

er, Birdie. This is getting way out of hand. There's no time even to mail out invitations.''

''I'll just put the announcement in this week's hotel newsletter. I trust you have something similar here? Good employee communications are so essential, don't you think?''

Was she questioning his management philosophy? If he wanted her to sell him the hotel, he didn't dare disagree. ''Well, yes, but...''

''Good! So we'll both invite our employees through our in-house newsletters, and you can invite the rest of your friends by phone. But first we have to set the time. Let's see... Kate said she wanted an evening wedding. Is seven o'clock all right?''

The time was the least of his concerns. ''Fine, but really, now, Birdie...''

She waved her hand and smiled indulgently. ''I know what you must be thinking—we haven't discussed the minister.''

The woman swung from topic to topic like a conversational trapeze artist, Richard thought in frustration. She was deliberately not letting him get a word in edgewise.

''Do you have someone selected?'' she asked now, not pausing long enough to let him draw a breath, much less form a thought.

He'd intended to ask a friend to impersonate a justice of the peace, but he couldn't very well tell her that. ''I've got a judge in mind. Now, back to the topic of...''

''Oh, no,'' Mrs. Delacroix interjected. ''A man of the cloth makes a marriage so much more sacred and binding, don't you think, Kate?''

''Well, yes, but...'' Kate began.

''See?'' Mrs. Delacroix turned to Richard with sly grin. ''Now, do you have a minister in mind?''

He was being railroaded, and he didn't like it one bit. ''I'll have one before the day is out,'' he said through clenched teeth.

''You needn't bother. I'll have the hotel's honorary chaplain officiate—it'll thrill him no end.'' She scooted forward on the

seat, preparing to rise. "There. Don't you feel better now that
the arrangements are all set?"

Better than what—a stiff at the morgue? Richard's stomach
felt as though he'd eaten some bad fish, and his head pounded
like a jackhammer. How the heck was he going to avoid a
marriage license and all the other legal requirements if Mrs.
Delacroix's handpicked minister presided at the ceremony?

Mrs. Delacroix answered the question for him. "I'm so
thrilled that a pair of newlyweds will be running the hotel,"
she said, clutching her enormous hot pink patent leather purse
as she rose from the chair. "I want to frame your marriage
certificate and hang it in the hotel foyer next to mine and
Louie's so our honeymooning guests will know you're newlyweds, too. Don't you think that's a splendid idea?"

Hell's bells and heaven's door knocker. He couldn't fake
the ceremony if the old dame was going to display the marriage certificate. She'd foiled him at every turn, and now he
was caught like a rat in a trap.

"Oh, dear. I almost forgot." Birdie opened her enormous
bag and extracted a document. "Here are the papers outlining
our agreement. I know you'll want to look them over, but in
a nutshell, they say I'll grant you complete ownership of the
hotel after you're married, if you operate it to my satisfaction
for thirty days." She held it out like forbidden fruit.

Richard reached out and took it. The papers felt seductively
smooth and cool in his hand.

Dadblast it—what a dilemma. The hotel was nearly within
his grasp. He wanted that place, and he wanted it bad.

But bad enough to go through with an actual marriage?

His grip tightened on the papers. The whole town would
think he and Kate were married anyway. Would it really make
much difference if they actually were? They could always get
an annulment later. And he'd make sure Kate got a generous
settlement for her trouble.

"You never did tell me what you thought about hanging
your marriage certificate in the foyer," Birdie said.

Richard stared down at the papers in his hand—papers that

could make his lifelong dream come true. He couldn't pass up this opportunity. He only hoped Kate would go along with it.

He curved his lips into what he hoped passed for a smile. "Great."

He glanced at Kate. Her blanched face told him she fully understood that their phony marriage had just escalated into the real thing.

Please, please, play along, he begged with his eyes. "I think it's a charming idea, don't you, Kate, darling?"

He didn't dare breathe during the long moment Kate hesitated.

"Charming," she finally echoed, her voice thin and weak.

He was so thrilled he nearly kissed her. He stopped himself just in time, remembering the impact she'd had on him in the garage yesterday.

Physical contact with Kate seemed to short out his brain waves. If he was going to make it through this nightmare, he'd better not touch her any more than necessary.

Mrs. Delacroix beamed. "Well, Kate, now all that remains is to find your wedding gown and a dress for your maid of honor. Why don't we go shopping tomorrow morning? Bring your maid of honor—I'll pick both of you up here at ten. That is, if you can persuade your boss here to give you some time off."

Mrs. Delacroix laughed as though she'd said something immensely witty, then swept out of the room as she'd come, leaving Richard feeling as if he'd just been run over by a hot pink bulldozer.

They were alone. Awareness of the fact settled around Kate as uncomfortably as a wet blanket in the wake of Mrs. Delacroix's silk-rustling, lavender-scented departure from Richard's office.

She and Richard normally worked alone, but she usually didn't feel this awkward and stiff and nervous. But then, she usually wasn't engaged to marry him in four days.

The thought made Kate's mouth go dry. She watched

Richard cross the room and shut the door, then seat himself beside her in the armchair Mrs. Delacroix had just vacated.

"This is getting a lot more complicated than I thought."

"No kidding."

"I can't tell you how much I appreciate this." His maple eyes were warm with gratitude. "I'll get my attorney to draw up an agreement guaranteeing it'll be more than worth your while. But, Kate…" He hesitated, his expression growing dark and serious. "If you don't want to go through with it, I'll understand."

Kate knew how much he wanted the hotel, knew how disappointed he'd be if she backed out now. That he was even offering her the opportunity to do so touched her heart.

If she had any sense, Kate thought, she'd take him up on the offer. All of her life she'd dreamed of her wedding day. She'd intended to marry only once, to a man who loved her as fully as she loved him. She didn't believe in deception, duplicity or marriages of convenience; she believed in true love, faithfulness and lifelong marriage.

But she also believed in never passing up a chance to help someone, and right now she had an opportunity to help two people at once. Richard couldn't buy the hotel without her help, and if he didn't buy it, Birdie would end up with her sentimental heart broken to bits when a big conglomerate razed her precious monument to true love.

When she looked at it in that light, she couldn't really see the harm. The only person at risk of getting hurt was her.

And she wouldn't, she thought adamantly—not as long as she kept in mind that it wasn't a real marriage. She was going into this with her eyes open. She knew Richard wasn't husband material, knew this was a temporary arrangement, knew it was a business affair, not an affair of the heart.

But a tiny, traitorous part of her felt like Cinderella going to the ball. And that tiny, traitorous part wanted to secretly pretend it might all have a happily-ever-after ending.

Which was the very reason she should back out now.

She should but she wouldn't. She could handle it, she re-assured herself.

She lifted her head to what she hoped was a jaunty angle. "What? And disappoint everyone who reads *The Times-Picayune?*"

Richard gave a rueful grin. "I'm sorry about how public this whole thing is becoming. When it's over, I'll take all the blame for the breakup."

Kate was glad he'd brought up the subject. The aftermath of this marriage was something they needed to address. "Will this have a lasting effect on my job? I mean, won't it seem odd that an ex-wife is working for her ex-husband?"

"Nah. We'll just tell everyone that we made an amicable split. They'll think we're exceptionally mature and sophisti-cated." Richard absently thumped the eraser end of a pencil on the arm of his chair. "Speaking of mature…we, uh, ought to lay down some ground rules. I want to set your mind at ease on a few scores."

"Such as?"

"Well, I have no expectations that this will be a marriage in the traditional sense. I mean, you don't have to worry that I… I mean, I won't expect…" He cleared his throat and looked away. "I'm sure you can figure out what I'm trying to say here."

Kate wished she were mature and sophisticated enough not to blush, but her cheeks burned all the same. "I understand perfectly."

He blew out a grateful breath. "Good."

She had no idea why his response left her so deflated. The clock on his credenza ticked loudly in the stilted silence. Kate laced her fingers tightly together in her lap and drew a deep breath. "While we're on the topic, for the month that we're, er, married…" The word felt alien on her tongue. Flustered, she looked down at her hands. "I mean, this is going to a pretty public wedding and all, and I…"

"Yes?"

The best way to say it was to just blurt it out. "Well, I don't think you should see any other women."

Richard chuckled, but his eyes were warm as they locked on hers. "You've got my word. I promise not to embarrass you." All traces of amusement left his face as another thought suddenly struck him. "I think that rule should apply to both of us, though."

She hadn't been on more than a handful of dates since she'd moved to New Orleans, and all of those had been set up by Annie and her fiancé. But it was flattering to have Richard think otherwise. "Oh—of course."

Still fiddling with the pencil, he gazed at her curiously. "Is there anything I need to know about the broken hearts you and Mrs. Delacroix were discussing?"

The only broken hearts in Kate's life belonged to a pair of kittens who'd tried to stow away in her purse when she'd volunteered at the SPCA last weekend, but she'd be darned if she'd tell him so. She didn't want him thinking she sat home alone every weekend evening and knitted.

Because she didn't. She sat home alone and watched old movies. She preferred that to going out with someone with whom she had no future, and she could usually determine that before a first date was halfway over. Annie said her standards were impossibly high, but Kate figured that when she met Mr. Right, she'd feel at least half as attracted to him as she was to her boss.

"Any boyfriends who're likely to make trouble?" he persisted. "Anyone who might stand up and object at the ceremony?"

The fact that Richard thought she might have such a devoted admirer made her suppress a smile. "I don't believe you have anything to worry about."

Richard leaned back in the chair and loosened his stranglehold on the pencil. "Well, good."

The silence grew awkward again. Kate cleared her throat. "There's one more thing we haven't discussed. What are our living arrangements going to be after the wedding?"

"I don't see why they have to be any different than they are now. I'll pick you up for work each morning, and we'll let Birdie think you've moved into my place. She'll never know we're not living together."

Kate swallowed back a vague sense of disappointment. "Well, what about a honeymoon? I'm sure she'll expect us to take one."

"Oh, hell—a honeymoon." Richard's sigh of dismay made her spirits plummet even farther. His face suddenly brightened. "We'll tell her we're delaying it—that we just can't wait to get settled in together. She'll think we're both going to my place after the wedding, but I'll drop you off at your apartment on the way."

Not exactly the wedding night of her dreams. Kate felt an irrational sense of irritation at his ready solution.

Well, if he could be so practical about this, she could, too. "I'll have to let my friend Annie in on things. She lives across the street, and if she doesn't know the marriage is a fake, she'll have marriage counselors paying house calls on our wedding night. She's an even bigger romantic than Mrs. Delacroix."

"I'll have to let my attorney know what's up, too. But other than that, we need to keep this quiet."

"As quiet as a three-hundred-guest wedding can be."

"I don't mean the wedding. I mean the fact that our marriage won't be consummated."

The word hung in the air, reverberating, and seemed to grow louder with each passing second.

Her cheeks flaming, Kate dropped her eyes. Her gaze fell on his thighs, toned from the five miles she knew he ran every morning. The muscles strained against the gray wool of his slacks in a way that made her mouth go dry.

In a real marriage, she'd feel those muscles strain against *her*. She'd see his runner's body naked, learn the texture of his skin, know the feel of his mouth on hers.

She abruptly pulled her gaze away, only to have it fall on his large tanned hands resting on the arm of the flame-stitched chair. In a real marriage, those hands would be moving over her body—peeling off her clothes, touching her, tracing the contours of her body. Her heart raced wildly at the thought.

But this wasn't a real marriage, she reminded herself, and it wouldn't be a real honeymoon—nor would she want it to be. Despite the annoying sense of attraction she felt toward him, Richard was not a good candidate for long-term matrimony.

He leaned forward, pulled his wallet out of his back pocket and extracted a platinum credit card. "Here—you'll need this. Charge your gown and whatever else you need for the wedding on it."

The idea of taking his personal credit card appalled her. "Oh, no, I don't want…"

He dropped the card on her lap. "You know I never let my employees pay for business expenses out of their own pocket."

She knew that, of course. There was absolutely no reason his words should cause such a lonely ache in her chest.

After all, this was strictly business, and she was nothing to Richard but an employee. She swallowed back the hard lump that had illogically formed in her throat and reminded herself to keep that firmly in mind.

The rest of the week passed in a flurry of activities—the shopping trip with Birdie and Annie, hours on the telephone issuing invitations, going with Richard for blood tests and the marriage license. Before Kate could believe it, it was Saturday evening, and Annie was fastening the last in the long row of tiny buttons that ran up the back of her wedding gown.

Kate's lanky, redheaded friend stepped back and sighed. "Oh, it's perfect."

And it was, Kate thought, turning to view herself in the three-way mirror in the hotel suite Birdie had provided as a dressing room.

She hardly recognized herself. The heavy cream silk of the gown skimmed her body all the way to the floor, accentuating curves she never knew she had. Thanks to the push-up bra

Annie had insisted on, she even had a hint of cleavage. The soft veil the hairdresser had fastened to her hair an hour earlier made her softly made-up face look dreamy and ethereal, like an old-fashioned soft-focus photo. She'd never dreamed she could look this good.

"Your parents would be so proud if they could see you now," Annie said, sighing.

The thought of her parents gave Kate a strange pang in her chest. "Would they?"

Filled with second thoughts, she turned to Annie, who had been her best friend since second grade. Annie had spent so much time at Kate's house when they were growing up in their small Ohio hometown that Kate's parents had referred to her as their second daughter. Annie knew how deeply Kate's parents had cared for each other, and how Kate had always longed for a marriage as close as theirs. She was the one person in the world Kate could count on for a straight answer. "Annie, am I doing the right thing?"

Annie smiled fondly. "You're following your heart, and you have the kindest, softest heart of anyone I know."

"Right," Kate said dryly. "The only thing softer is my head."

Annie's brows puckered in concern. "You don't have to go through with this, you know."

Kate sighed. "I don't want to let Richard down, and I don't want a big conglomerate to tear down Birdie's hotel. Besides, I gave my word."

"No one would blame you for changing your mind."

"I would blame myself. I've never gone back on my word before, and I don't intend to start now." There was another, secret reason she wouldn't admit, not even to Annie. If she backed out now, she'd be admitting that the attraction she felt for Richard was getting the best of her. She was determined not to give in to such an irrational emotion. "Besides, buying this hotel means a lot to Richard. It's the only thing I've ever seen him get sentimental over."

"He's likely to get plenty sentimental when he gets a load

of you in that dress. I wouldn't be surprised if he falls in a dead faint.''

Kate rolled her eyes. "If he faints, it'll be over the fact that he's about to become a married man. I've never seen anyone more opposed to matrimony in my life.''

Annie twirled her engagement ring. "I don't know. My Steven was pretty thoroughly opposed, and he's poised to take the plunge in just three more months.''

Kate grinned. "Steven never stood a chance. His single days were numbered from the day you two met.''

"What makes you say that?''

"Gee, I don't know. Maybe the way you stalked him like a big-game hunter.''

Annie smiled impishly. "All I did was move to New Orleans when he got transferred.''

"Uh-huh. And rent the other half of the duplex where he was living.''

"Double. In New Orleans, duplexes are called doubles.''

Kate was not to be diverted. "And let's not forget how you shamelessly sent yourself flowers and balloons and singing telegrams, which always conveniently arrived when you weren't at home so Steven had to accept delivery. The poor guy was terrified you were about to marry someone else.''

Annie's mischievous smile widened. "I got my man, didn't I? And I've got a strong feeling you're about to get yours. I'll bet Richard won't last the month without wanting to make this pseudomarriage the real thing.''

"In your dreams, Canfield.''

Annie gave a knowing look. "From the way your eyes light up every time you talk about him, I'd say it was more in yours.''

Were her feelings that transparent? Kate had never admitted to anyone, not even to Annie, how she really felt about Richard. She tried her best not even to admit it to herself.

"Don't be ridiculous.'' Kate turned away from her friend's gaze and pretended to adjust her veil. "So what's your real opinion of what I'm doing?''

"The truth?"

"Yes."

Annie grinned owlishly. "I think it's great. The most eligible bachelor in New Orleans is going to be exclusively yours for the next month. You'll have the perfect opportunity to reel him in."

"Who said anything about my wanting to reel him in?"

"No one. But no one needed to."

Kate stepped away from the mirror and glanced at Annie reprovingly. "Just because you've got stars in your eyes doesn't mean I do, too."

"You're not fooling me, McCormick. But it's your wedding day, so I won't argue with you about it." Annie reached for a hairbrush and took Kate's place in front of the mirror. "Besides, even if things don't work out between you and Richard, this marriage is still a great idea. Your marketability is going to skyrocket."

"What on earth are you talking about?"

Annie flicked the brush through her short auburn hair. "Every man in New Orleans is going to be intrigued by the woman who managed to rope Richard Chandler into marriage, only to boot him out a month later. You're going to attract the cream of the crop, kiddo. It couldn't be more brilliant if I'd planned it myself."

Kate shook her head. "If you weren't a marketing consultant, you'd probably be plotting the overthrow of foreign governments. You're a dangerous woman, Canfield." She smiled fondly at her friend. "And you look it in that dress. Emerald is definitely your color."

Annie set her long silk gown to whirling. "Thanks for picking out a flattering dress. I'll be sure and return the favor."

Kate's reply was cut short as the door creaked open and Mrs. Delacroix bustled in. She wore her trademark bright pink, this time in flowing, floor-length chiffon. Her platinum hair towered over her head in an elaborate arrangement accented with a garish scattering of rhinestones and bows. Her blue eyes sparkled like her diamond necklace as she caught sight of

Kate. "Oh, my!" She clasped her ring-encrusted fingers together in an expression of ecstacy. "You're a vision of loveliness. You'll knock Richard's socks off!"

A rush of anxiety flooded Kate's chest. This would be the first time he'd ever seen her in anything except business attire. She tried to tell herself that his opinion of her appearance didn't matter in the least, but deep inside it mattered far too much for comfort.

Birdie turned toward Annie. She'd taken an instant liking to Kate's maid of honor on the shopping expedition—which wasn't surprising, Kate thought wryly, since they were two meddlesome peas in a pod. "And look at you, dear. You're absolutely breathtaking!"

"Thank you. You're quite a sight yourself."

Kate smiled at Annie's tactful choice of words.

"Did you take care of that little matter for me?" the elderly woman asked.

"It's all handled," Annie replied.

"Good."

Something was up, and it heightened Kate's sense of nervousness. "What little matter are you talking about?"

"Oh, nothing—nothing at all." Mrs. Delacroix glanced at her diamond wristwatch in what Kate was certain was a deliberate attempt to change the subject. "Oh, look at the time! We need to head downstairs. Annie, dear, do you remember the way to take Kate to the ballroom using the back hallway?"

Annie nodded. "I'll make sure she makes a grand entrance."

"We should get going, then. The guests are all seated, and the groom is waiting."

A million butterflies suddenly took wing in Kate's stomach. In just a few moments, she'd be married to Richard.

The older woman turned to Kate. "Are you still sure you want to walk down the aisle alone? I can accompany you, if you like."

Kate smiled, touched by the old woman's offer. "That's very sweet, but I'll be fine."

"All right, then. I'll go take my seat." Birdie kissed Kate on the cheek, then turned at the door. "Just think—the next time we talk, you'll be Mrs. Richard Chandler."

Mrs. Richard Chandler. The thought made Kate's hands tremble as she bent and draped her train over her arm.

Annie picked up the two bouquets from a side table. "Ready?"

Kate mustered a smile. "As ready as I'll ever be." She followed Annie down the hall and into a service elevator, her courage wavering. She sought for something, anything, to think about that might keep the butterflies in her stomach under control. "What was the favor Birdie asked you to do?"

Annie looked evasive. "I can't say. It's a surprise."

"I don't need any more surprises. It's enough of a surprise to find myself about to walk down the aisle to marry Richard."

"But I promised Birdie I wouldn't tell you."

The elevator doors opened into a service corridor before Kate could question her further. The soft strains of a string quartet wafted through a service door. Kate's palms grew damp as she recognized the beautiful melody of the sonata she'd selected.

"That's the ballroom," Annie said excitedly. She stepped up to the door, cracked it open and peered in. "Oh, Kate—come look. Everything looks wonderful. It's just like you used to describe when we were little girls dreaming about our weddings."

Kate couldn't resist. She stepped to the door and peeked through the opening.

"You're right," she murmured. Candles shimmered in tall candelabra. Elegantly attired guests sat in long rows of white-covered chairs. A white satin runner ran from the back of the ballroom to the front, stopping before a flower-flanked altar. White roses and gardenias were everywhere, scenting the air with an intoxicating fragrance.

It was her fondest fantasy come to life—except that it wasn't real. There would be no marriage, no anniversaries, no happily ever after—no wedding night, no honeymoon, no ardent bridegroom who couldn't wait to get her alone. When the ceremony and reception were over, she'd be back in her small uptown apartment, alone in her single bed.

It was a sobering thought. All the same, it was hard to suppress a ripple of excitement as she gazed at the picture-perfect scene. She stepped back from the doorway and forced herself to remain outwardly calm. "Come on, Annie. We'd better stop lurking in the hallway and take our places, or we'll miss our big moment."

They made their way out of the service corridor and into the ballroom foyer. Kate tried to slow her racing pulse by focusing her thoughts on their earlier conversation as Annie arranged the train of her gown behind her.

"Okay, now. You're my maid of honor, so do the honorable thing and tell me what Birdie's surprise is."

Annie finished smoothing the length of silk, then straightened and brushed a strand of auburn hair from her eyes. "Are you sure you want to know?"

"Sure I'm sure." The orchestra ended the song. Kate's stomach knotted. At any moment, the pianist would strike up the chords of the wedding march. "What's the big secret?"

Annie sighed and handed her the bridal bouquet. "Birdie had me pack an overnight bag for you."

"Why?"

"She thinks the new owners of the Honeymoon Hotel should spend their wedding night here. She's reserved the most luxurious suite for you and Richard."

Kate's heart thudded wildly against her ribs. "But—but you know the situation, Annie!"

Annie raised her shoulders apologetically. "I know, I know, but I had no choice. She wouldn't take no for an answer. There's no way she's going to let you and Richard leave this hotel tonight, and you can't very well sleep in your wedding gown. I figured that if I didn't pack you a bag, you'd have nothing to wear tonight." Her face creased in a mischievous grin. "Which might not be such a bad idea, now that I think of it. After all, Richard's a real hunk, and you're obviously crazy about him. And it *is* your wedding night.''

''No, it's not. Not really. Not like that!''

The opening strains of the wedding march resounded from the room. Annie patted her hand and smiled. ''You never know. If you play your cards right, it just might be.'' Two ushers threw open the double doors. ''That's my cue. See you down front.'' With a wide grin, Annie turned and started down the aisle.

Kate watched her friend gracefully make her way to the front of the ballroom, then drew a deep breath. It was her turn to make the long walk. She stared out, vaguely aware that three hundred faces were turned toward her. And then she saw the face she was looking for, gazing at her from the front of the altar, and she had eyes for no one else.

Richard. Her heart thumped so hard she thought it would burst. He was staring back at her, handsome as the devil in black-tie, wearing a stunned expression on his incredibly handsome face.

She started toward him, her emotions in turmoil, once again feeling more than a little like Cinderella. She knew this was only temporary, that next month the clock would strike midnight and her life would resume its normal pattern. But right now, all she could think about was the magic of the moment, and all she could feel was an odd mix of anxiety and anticipation over what the night might bring.

Chapter Four

"I now pronounce you husband and wife. You may kiss the bride."

Richard drew a deep breath. The way Kate had looked in that dress as she'd sashayed down the aisle had nearly given him a heart attack. He'd always thought wedding gowns made women look like shapeless blobs of lace, but Kate's dress clung to every curve—and boy, did she have some curves to cling to. He'd discovered as much when he picked her up in that parking garage, and he'd been giving the matter far too much thought ever since. But even in his wildest imaginings, he'd had no idea that Kate was hiding such a sweet little body under all her bulky jackets. She was small-boned and slight and ladylike—completely different from the tall, chesty blondes he usually preferred, but just as deliciously feminine. She was enough to make him rethink his position on the ideal female form.

He'd avoided looking at her as much as possible during the ceremony as a matter of self-preservation, but he couldn't avoid her any longer. Three hundred guests were gazing at him expectantly, waiting for him to kiss her.

He swallowed hard and turned toward her. Good Lord. She was gorgeous—flat-out, drop-dead gorgeous. Her skin looked as flawless as the gardenia blossoms she was clutching, her eyes were a heartbreaking shade of green and her lips were enough to tempt a saint.

"You're supposed to kiss me," she whispered.

Too late, he realized he'd been standing there like a fool, staring at her for an inordinately long amount of time. He gulped again, put his arms around her and set himself to the task.

Soft. It was his last coherent thought as he slid into a steamy whirlpool of sensation. Her lips were jarringly soft, joltingly alive, shockingly warm. So were her slight breasts pressed against the lapels of his tuxedo. He was vaguely aware of the pressure of her arms around his neck, of the scent of her heady perfume, of the heat of her breath against his face—but the thing that capsized his senses was the soft slide of her lips under his own.

She tasted faintly like the ocean—salty and rich and wet. Her mouth pulsed with promises and possibilities and deep, dark secrets he longed to explore. When her lips parted and moved under his, a wave of pleasure crashed over him. He tightened his hold on her, bent her over backward and kissed her until he was breathless and drowning, completely swept away in a hot, swift current of desire.

A soft tittering sound filtered through the loud pounding of his pulse in his ears. He heard a man behind him clear his throat, then felt a tap on his shoulder. "I think you'd better save the rest of this for tonight, son."

He opened his eyes to see the minister leaning over him, his kindly face wearing an amused expression. Richard rapidly glanced down at Kate. She was bent backward over his arm, her lips red and kiss-swollen, her cheeks pink and bright, her half-opened eyes dazed and dreamy.

Holy cow—had he completely lost his mind? He'd completely lost his head, that was for sure.

He straightened, pulling Kate into an upright position along with him. She clung to his neck as if her legs had morphed into al dente spaghetti. "Are you all right?" he whispered.

The strains of the recessional resounded through the room. She dropped her arms as well as her eyes, nodded, then wobbled slightly as she turned around. Annie stepped forward and straightened the train of her gown behind her. Richard held out his arm, and Kate paused before gingerly placing her hand on it, hesitating as if she were afraid to touch him.

Well, no wonder—she probably thought he was likely to throw her over his shoulder and tote her off like a caveman after that Conan the Barbarian kiss. Chagrined, Richard marched down the aisle at a rapid clip, anxious to have the whole ceremony over with. As he guided Kate past the first row of guests, he caught sight of Mrs. Delacroix, smiling mistily and dabbing her eyes with a lace handkerchief.

The sight nearly made him falter. At least there was an unexpected benefit to his overly enthusiastic behavior—Birdie thought she'd just witnessed a kiss of true love. He couldn't have staged anything more convincing if he'd planned it.

But he hadn't planned it, and that was precisely why it bothered him. It had been a spontaneous, impetuous act, completely at odds with his usual modus operandi. He prided himself on his ability to think clearly under pressure, to keep his cool, to handle difficult situations with aplomb. It was what he privately thought of as his winner's edge. He couldn't afford to lose it now, not when he had all his assets on the line in the biggest gamble of his career.

The weight of the risk suddenly weighed heavily on his shoulders. So did the significance of what he'd just done. His mouth dry, he glanced sideways at his new wife. *His wife.* Of all the things he'd ever envisioned having, a lawfully wedded wife wasn't one of them.

A sudden tightening in his throat threatened to choke off his air supply. The last thing he'd ever intended to do was get married. If he didn't believe so strongly in never second-guessing himself, he'd be tempted to think he'd made a terrible mistake, that he should have backed off when Birdie forced the issue of the wedding license.

But this was no time to start playing Monday-morning quarterback, he told himself sternly. He'd done what he had to do to get the hotel.

Besides, they weren't *really* married. As long as they didn't consummate the marriage, they'd have grounds for an annulment. His attorney had already checked it out.

There was no reason to be so riddled with sudden anxiety, he silently assured himself. This was Kate—good old reliable Kate, his loyal, trustworthy secretary with a heart as big as Alaska, who'd been known to give her lunch to street bums, who put coins in expired parking meters so strangers wouldn't get parking tickets. He spent more time with Kate in the course of an average day than he spent with any other human being, and he knew her as well or better than he'd ever known anyone.

So why did she all of a sudden seem like a total stranger? How come he'd never really noticed how attractive she was before? And why the heck had kissing her thrown him into such a mind-numbing state of complete engrossment that he'd completely forgotten his surroundings, his manners and probably even his own name?

"That was some kiss," Annie whispered to Kate half an hour later as the receiving line broke up and Richard went to have a word with his best man, Harvey Evans, a middle-age real-estate appraiser who frequently worked for him. "Didn't seem very platonic to me."

It hadn't felt very platonic, either. In fact, Kate had never experienced anything so bone-meltingly nonplatonic in her life. She still hadn't quite recovered from it. "I'm sure he was just trying to look convincing."

Annie grinned. "Well, he convinced me all right. Looked like you were more than a little convinced yourself."

Convinced she'd died and gone to heaven, Kate thought ruefully. When Richard's lips had met hers, she'd heard bells and seen paradise. She'd lost all ability to think or reason or move, except to try to get closer to Richard.

Had he felt it, too? It seemed impossible that anything so earthshaking could be one-sided. But maybe it had just seemed that way because she'd fantasized about it for so long.

She glanced over at her groom. He was still involved in an earnest conversation with Harvey. About business, no doubt.

The thought popped all of her illusions like a straight pin in a balloon. Any man who would discuss business at his own wedding was not a man who was likely to get carried away by his emotions, she thought ruefully. She might have found that kiss to be the most exciting, sense-shattering experience of her life, but Richard no doubt considered it nothing more than a necessary part of the marriage charade.

"If that's how he kisses you in front of a crowd, I can't wait to find out what happens when you're alone in that hotel room," Annie whispered.

The thought of spending the night alone with him made Kate's mouth go dry. Before she could form a reply, Birdie hustled over, Richard in tow. "It's time for you two to take your places at the head table."

Richard took Kate's arm and steered her across the room. "The sooner we get this started, the sooner we'll get it over with," he muttered under his breath as she seated herself in the chair he held out for her.

"Not as soon as you might think," Kate warned.

What the heck did she mean by that? Richard frowned, but before he could ask her to explain, a tuxedoed waiter bustled between them, filling the crystal stemware with champagne. The next thing he knew, his best man was on his feet, holding his glass aloft.

"Most of us in this room never thought we'd see the day when Richard Chandler would tie the knot, but one look at his beautiful bride and it's easy to see why he changed his mind about marriage. Richard, Kate..." Harvey inclined his glass toward them. "May your marriage be long and happy, filled with the same rich joy I've found in my own."

A stab of guilt shot through Richard. He knew Harvey's whole world revolved around his wife and family, and he hated the thought of deceiving his old friend. He forced a smile and looked out at the roomful of upturned faces. Most of the guests were hotel employees, people he didn't even know, yet their eyes were filled with warm wishes. He smiled and nodded and took a sip, but the champagne tasted bitter on his tongue. He didn't like the idea of perpetrating a hoax on this well-meaning crowd any more than he liked tricking his friend.

But the end justified the means, he told himself. It was the only way that ditzy Delacroix dame was going to sell him the hotel.

Richard realized the entire room was looking at him expectantly, waiting for him to make the traditional groom's toast to the bride. He stood, held up his glass and looked at Kate, then swallowed hard. This would be a whole lot easier if she didn't look like a blasted angel, he thought grimly. Of all the people he hated deceiving, Kate bothered him the most. If she knew his true plans for the hotel, she never would have consented to this scheme.

The thought made it hard for him to look her in the eye. "To Kate—who made me the happiest man on earth when she agreed to marry me." That much, at least, was the truth.

Another kiss was in order, but he didn't dare risk anything more than a peck on the cheek. Even so, he felt it again—a chemical reaction strong enough to need EPA regulation, heating his blood like a butane burner on a test tube. He managed to lower himself back in his seat, hoping he didn't look as foggy-headed as he felt.

Dammit, this was insane. This was Kate, for Pete's sake— the woman he'd worked with on a daily basis for the past eight months, whose primary virtue up until last week had been the way she efficiently handled things while seeming virtually invisible. Why was his libido suddenly stuck in overdrive every time he touched her?

Stress—that must be the problem. Stress could do strange things to a person.

Well, stress or no stress, he was honor-bound not to act on this insane attraction. His conscience was bothering him about this whole setup as it was, and he didn't want to take advantage of the situation. He'd promised Kate as much, and he intended to keep his word.

He chugged down the last of his champagne and cast a wary eye sideways at the source of his distress. Kate was laughing at something Harvey had just said to her, her face lit up as if a spotlight were shining on it. Good heavens, she was lovely. He didn't know whether to feel proud as punch or irritated as hell, and ended up feeling a little of both.

He ran a finger around his wing collar, wishing he could unbutton the suddenly too-tight contraption. He couldn't wait until this whole ordeal was over and he could drop Kate off at her apartment. He'd go home, take a long, cold shower and get a good night's sleep—and the next time he saw Kate, she'd be out of that eye-popping dress and back into one of her usual suits of armor. Surely then his feelings about her would settle back to normal.

Birdie bobbed to her feet. "It's my turn to offer a toast to the newlyweds. As I'm sure everyone knows, they'll soon be managing the hotel, and if all goes well, in a month they'll be the new owners. In light of that, I've arranged a little surprise." Birdie lifted her glass and paused melodramatically. Judging from the smile on her face, the old gal was quite pleased with herself. "Richard, Kate—here's to another lifelong marriage that begins with a wedding night at the Honeymoon Hotel."

Richard's smile hardened and froze like packed snow. It was all he could do to maintain his composure as the roomful of people cheered.

Hell's bells. He couldn't refuse Birdie's offer right now without looking like the worst kind of heel. "I'll get us out of this," he promised Kate in a low whisper. "I'll talk to her. Don't worry."

* * *

"I take it your little talk with Birdie didn't go as you planned?" Kate asked three hours later.

"You might say that." Richard closed the door to the suite they'd just entered and leaned against it with a heavy sigh.

It had taken a while to find the opportunity to talk to Birdie. First he'd had to survive the excruciatingly long dinner, then he'd had to endure an even more excruciating dance with Kate—a lengthy torment where his need to keep his distance in order to keep his head had warred with the urge to pull her flush against him and milk the role of besotted bridegroom for all it was worth.

Next he'd fulfilled the obligatory dance with the maid of honor, talked with an endless stream of well-wishers, and then, finally, he'd asked Birdie to dance.

The old gal had been surprisingly light on her feet. "What do you think of my surprise?" she'd asked as she twirled back into his arms after executing a graceful pirouette.

Richard had searched for a tactful response. "It's very…thoughtful. But I'm afraid Kate and I are going to have to decline."

Birdie's mouth had puckered as she frowned. "Oh, you can't! I've got everything all arranged. I had Harvey and Annie bring toiletries and a change of clothes for each of you, and your bags are already in your room. Besides, the employees are expecting it."

"The employees will never know the difference."

"Of course they will. They have a grapevine that rivals the Internet. The security guards and doormen know who comes and goes from all the entrances, and the housekeeping and front office staffs know all about who's in what room."

Richard shot her his most charming smile and lowered his voice conspiratorially, hoping to appeal to her overdeveloped sense of romance. "The fact of the matter is, Birdie, I've always dreamed of taking my bride home on my wedding night. I can't wait to pick her up and carry her across the threshold. It's a secret fantasy of mine."

Birdie chuckled appreciatively, but she didn't bite at the

sentimental bait. "I'm sure you'll have more than enough of your fantasies fulfilled tonight. No point in cramming too much into one day." She laughed again, making her multiple chins jiggle like Jell-O. "Besides, homecoming should be just as special as your wedding. You'll appreciate it more if it's a whole separate event."

He'd obviously made a miscalculation. Maybe Birdie needed to be handled more firmly. "We appreciate your generosity, Birdie, but Kate and I want to do this our way."

"If you want to buy the Honeymoon Hotel, I'm afraid I really must insist." Her tone was still pleasant, but it was undergirded by a note of pure steel. Her eyes held a tough, unyielding message, as well. "You're taking over a hotel that caters to newlyweds, Richard. As a newlywed yourself, it's your obligation to stay here. You don't want to imply that the hotel isn't good enough for your own wedding night, do you?"

"Of course not!"

"I didn't think so. And I'm sure you don't want anyone to get the mistaken impression that you are." Her face had creased into a smile, and she'd sighed contentedly. "I'm so glad it's all settled. I'd hate to sell my hotel to anyone besides you two."

Richard's muscles had tensed until they felt like petrified wood, but he'd decided against pursuing the issue further. It wasn't worth the risk. After all, it was only for one night.

So now here he was, locked up with the woman he'd looked forward to getting away from all evening—the woman who'd made the cake-cutting, garter-tossing, smiling-till-his-face-ached ordeal excruciating by transforming herself into the sexiest bride he'd ever seen.

Why the heck had she picked a dress like that, anyway? he wondered irritably, watching her cross the elegantly furnished room. Brides were supposed to look sweet and innocent, not luscious as ripe fruit.

She seemed completely unconscious of the effect she was having on him, and annoyingly at ease with the whole discomfitting situation. He watched her look around the living room with the casual fascination of a tourist on a plantation tour.

"Looks like someone besides Birdie decorated the suites," she said, running her hand along the back of a cream-colored brocade sofa.

Richard nodded and pushed off the door. "When I toured the property before making my offer on the hotel, Birdie told me her husband had insisted on hiring a professional designer to do the guest rooms. Wanted to save her from having to do all the work, she said. My guess is the old guy didn't want the guests suffering from eyestrain."

Which was one of the problems he was suffering from right now, but for an entirely different reason. He was going to wear out his eyeballs if he couldn't stop staring at Kate.

She laughed, then crossed the room and peered into the bedroom. "Wow. A tester bed. And it looks like an antique!"

"It is. Several of the suites are furnished with them."

"I've always wondered why they call them testers."

Richard had no trouble imagining why. The way Kate looked in that dress made him want to give it a test right now.

He breathed a sigh of relief as she closed the bedroom door, only to feel another rush of anxiety as she lowered herself to the sofa. The neckline of her dress plunged slightly, offering a shadowy hint of cleavage.

The temperature in the room suddenly soared. Richard yanked off his bow tie, loosened his shirt and stalked to the thermostat on the far wall. "I'll bet you're anxious to get out of that dress," he remarked, flipping the air conditioner to high.

Blast. That hadn't come out right at all. He immediately tried to set the record straight. "I mean, you probably want to slip into something more comfortable."

Hell, that sounded even worse. He jammed a hand in his thick hair. "I mean jeans or slacks. Something not so…" *For Pete's sake, Chandler—don't say provocative!* "…tight fitting," he finished lamely.

She leaned back against the plump cushions, causing her neckline to dip still farther as the fabric strained against her breasts. "Actually, this is pretty comfortable."

Not for me, it isn't. He cleared his throat. "Well, as late as it is, maybe we should just get ready for bed."

Oh, good one, Chandler. What the hell was the matter with him? He was handling this conversation with the finesse of a dentist drilling teeth with a jackhammer.

Kate looked down and studied her manicure. "Actually, I think I'm too keyed up to sleep."

Richard shoved his hands in his pockets and shifted his stance. "Maybe a drink would help." He could sure use a good stiff one himself.

"I'd love some mineral water, if we have any."

Richard strode across the living room toward the bar, then stopped short as his eyes landed on an array of gleaming silver platters arranged on a long rosewood table. Peeled shrimp, oysters on the half shell, exotic fruits, a bowl of black caviar and a tray of chocolate-dipped strawberries sat beside an iced magnum of Dom Pérignon. "I don't know about mineral water, but it looks like we've got just about anything else you might want. Come get a load of this."

Kate unfolded her feet, rose and crossed the room to join him. "Looks like Birdie thought we'd work up an appetite."

"Well, we'd better not disappoint her." Holy Moses, he'd done it again. He couldn't seem to open his mouth without inserting his foot right in it. "About the food and champagne, I mean," he added rapidly, pulling the bottle from its icy nest and peeling the foil from the cork.

Kate studied the fruit. "Do you think she suspects we're trying to trick her?"

Richard froze, the bottle in his hand. "Why? Do you?"

Kate shrugged and speared a slice of mango. "I don't know. She's asked a few questions that made me wonder. When we went shopping, for example, she asked about your family. If you hadn't told me about your parents' divorce, I would have really been put on the spot."

A feeling of uneasiness gripped Richard's chest. After going to the extreme of getting married, he didn't intend to have this deal fall through. He recalled how Birdie had quizzed him on the topic of Kate's family, and his sense of trepidation heightened. "I guess I ought to learn more about your family in case she decides to question me, too."

"Might not be a bad idea."

He expertly popped the cork, sending it flying across the room. His thoughts too, flew, back to the first time he'd met Kate. He distinctly remembered it. He'd been impressed by her cover letter and résumé, and he'd been even more impressed when she'd walked through his office door, the picture of professionalism in a no-nonsense dark suit.

Since he'd already interviewed a dozen unsuitable applicants, Kate had stood out as a real find. She'd come across as intelligent, competent and reliable, and her references had been glowing. He remembered feeling an intense sense of relief at finding her, but he'd be darned if he could remember the particulars of why she'd been in the market for a job in the first place.

He splashed champagne into two fluted glasses and glanced at her. "I know you worked for an insurance firm in a small town in Ohio before you came to work for me. But why were you job hunting in New Orleans?"

"I fell in love with the city when I came to visit Annie."

"So you just decided to up and move?"

Kate placed a strawberry on her plate and shrugged. "The man I'd been working for was getting ready to retire, so I was already in the market for a new job. And I'd just ended a relationship, so I thought a change of scene might do me good."

A relationship. The information left Richard oddly unsettled. He knew he was getting into territory that was none of his business—after all, Birdie would almost certainly never ask him about his wife's former boyfriends—but curiosity was burning a hole in him. Was this the one long-term relationship Kate had referred to earlier? He pretended to concentrate on selecting an oyster in an effort to disguise his avid interest. "What happened? With the relationship, I mean."

"I broke it off."

"Why?"

She shrugged. "We wanted different things out of life."

"What did you want?"

"Marriage to someone who makes my heart race."

"And this guy didn't want to get married?"

"Actually, he did. But he didn't affect my pulse rate." *Unlike you,* Kate silently added.

Mercy, what was she doing, carrying on about something so emotional? Richard would think she was as irrational as Birdie. "I've seen what a good marriage can be like, and I don't want to settle for less," she hurried to explain. "I want one like my parents had. They were best friends and business partners, but there was some kind of magic between them, too. Sometimes they'd look at each other and I'd get the feeling they were having a whole conversation no one else could hear."

Richard eyed her dubiously. "I hate to tell you this, but marriages like that are harder to come by than winning lottery tickets. What else do you want?"

"A home. Children. A houseful of pets." She gave a wry grin. "That was another reason I broke off with Morton. He didn't like my cat."

"You have a cat?"

"He died a few months ago. I'd had him for twelve years."

Her eyes looked so forlorn Richard regretted bringing up the topic. "Gee, I'm sorry to hear it." He shifted uneasily. "Do you have any other pets?"

"No. I plan to get another cat eventually, but for the time being, I'm getting my animal fix by volunteering one weekend a month at the local animal shelter." She flashed a rueful smile. "To tell you the truth, I miss Mr. Bojangles a whole lot more than I miss Morton."

"Morton—that was the guy's name? No wonder you preferred the cat."

Kate grinned as Richard pulled out a chair at the end of the rosewood table for her. She lowered herself into it and accepted a glass of champagne.

He sat down beside her. "What kind of business did your parents have?"

"A pharmacy. It was the only one in town."

"That must have provided your family with a good living."

"Not exactly."

Richard raised a quizzical eyebrow. "If it wasn't profitable, why didn't they sell it?"

"It had been in Dad's family for three generations. He felt an obligation to keep it open. Partly because his parents would have wanted him to, but also because the townspeople needed a local drugstore."

Richard's forehead creased. "But I don't understand. If it didn't have any competition, it should have made a killing."

Kate took a sip of champagne. "Dad couldn't bear to see someone go without medicine just because they couldn't afford it. Most of the profits went to providing free drugs for people who needed them."

"Wow. What did your mom think of that?"

Kate smiled. "She thought he was the most wonderful man in the world. He was her hero."

Richard let out a low whistle. "My mother would have killed my old man for giving away his profits. Of course, that never would have happened, because Dad wasn't given to acts of generosity. 'Let the bums earn their own way like I did,' he used to say."

"My dad used to say just the opposite," Kate said softly. "He always said we should share our blessings, because we were the richest people he knew."

Richard frowned. "But you just said the pharmacy barely made a profit."

Kate's eyes were soft. "Dad wasn't talking about money."

Her words hit Richard like a blow to the solar plexus. He was an idiot, he thought in disgust. Kate's values were based on things beside money, things he knew darned little about.

An odd feeling of wistfulness washed over him. He took a deep gulp from his glass, feeling lower than the tail of a crawfish. "Sounds like you and I were raised on different planets," he said gruffly.

Different planets? More like different solar systems. He had no business talking a woman like Kate into marrying him just so he could turn a profit. He was a real jerk, putting her in a situation like this.

He cleared his throat uneasily, searching for something neutral to say. "It sounds like your folks were well suited to each other."

"They were. Mom used to say that each of us has a soul mate—someone we're intended to spend our lives with. She believed that divine providence always brings couples together."

"Oh, yeah? How did she explain all the unhappy marriages out there?"

"She said some people don't know how to give or receive love, and others don't recognize their better half when they meet. Mom used to say she and Dad were lucky because they both knew they'd met their match from the moment they laid eyes on each other."

"Do you believe that, too? That you've got a soul mate out there somewhere?"

"Yes." Kate glanced down at her plate. "At least, I sure hope so."

It figured, Richard thought. But somehow it didn't strike him as being as corny a concept as he would have imagined—not after hearing about Kate's parents. He stared at her pensively. "What you told Birdie about your parents' car crash…that was the truth?"

Pain glazed her eyes, making him regret bringing up the subject. "Yes. I was eighteen. Mom was killed immediately. Dad died a few days later, even though his injuries shouldn't have been fatal. The doctors said he lost his will to live. I think he died of a broken heart."

Tears pooled in her eyes. Instinctively, Richard reached out and took her hand. It felt small and soft and fragile in his palm. The wedding band he'd placed on it earlier glimmered in the lamplight, a tiny beacon of reproach.

No wonder she put such a high premium on love and marriage, coming from a home like that. A fresh stab of guilt shot through him.

"That must have been awful for you," he said, not knowing how to comfort her but feeling compelled to try.

She nodded, her throat moving convulsively. "I really missed them today. I know this isn't a real marriage or anything, but I used to dream about my wedding day. I'd always imagined walking down the aisle on my father's arm, and seeing my mom seated in the front aisle, and..." Her voice wavered, then cracked. A tear slid down her cheek.

Hell's bells—he felt like a life-form lower than plankton. He reached out and gently wiped away the tear with his free hand. "Kate, I'm so sorry."

"No, *I'm* sorry. I didn't mean to get all sentimental." Her eyes were brimming, but she still managed a tremulous smile. "Don't pay any attention to me. I always cry at weddings."

It wasn't just the tears that got to him—it was that brave, shaky smile. He wiped away another teardrop with the pad of his thumb. "I didn't know about your family and how strongly you felt about marriage when I asked you to do this. I wouldn't have asked if I'd known. Why didn't you tell me?"

Kate blinked hard, desperately trying to corral her emotions, knowing how he hated emotional scenes, hating the thought that she was staging one. "Well, this isn't really a marriage—not in the true sense of the word, anyway. I didn't expect to get all mushy about it."

She wiped her eyes, and when her vision cleared, the eyes gazing into hers were so dark and troubled that the sight of them squeezed her heart. She realized he was squeezing her hand, as well, and she returned the pressure. "You didn't force me into this," she told him earnestly. "It was my decision. And it'll be more than worth it if it helps you and Birdie."

Especially you, she added silently. The things he'd told her about his childhood echoed in her mind, conjuring up cold, lonely images of a love-starved little boy seeking refuge at his uncle's hotel, trying to forget the turmoil at home by losing himself in hotel chores. The image stood in stark contrast to her own memories of a sunny, love-drenched youth, of smiling parents, of a home filled with unconditional love.

No wonder Richard seemed so aloof, so inaccessible, so work-driven, Kate thought, her heart flooding with sympathy. If owning and operating this hotel could give him just a little of the warmth and sense of belonging that was lacking in his life, she was more than glad to help.

His eyes held something she couldn't quite name, something that made her acutely conscious of the pressure of his hand on hers, of his palm still cupping her cheek. "You're one nice lady, Mrs. Chandler."

Mrs. Chandler. The name sent goose bumps chasing up her spine, along with a keen awareness that they were legally married, this was their wedding night, that they were alone in a dimly lit honeymoon suite.

The memory of the way he'd kissed her when the minister had proclaimed them husband and wife blazed a trail of heat through her belly.

"You're the nicest person I've ever met, much less ever married," he said. His half-teasing tone held an undernote of seriousness that took her breath away. "That soul mate of yours is going to be one lucky guy."

Kate gazed into his eyes, and as she did, something shifted and changed between them, like a river surging around a bend, picking up strength and momentum, carving out a deeper channel.

His hand moved from her cheek to her hair. "You make a beautiful bride. I could hardly repeat my vows during the ceremony, I was so bowled over by the sight of you in that dress."

Kate's heart hammered in her chest. She couldn't speak. She couldn't think. She could do nothing but stare at him and remember how that kiss had felt.

His hand slid around the back of her head, pulling her forward. Her eyes fastened on his lips. The hard-soft feel of his mouth, the gentle-rough rasp of his clean-shaven jaw, replayed in her mind like a slow motion scene from a movie. She wanted to relive it. She was dying to relive it. She leaned toward him, her lips yearning, her pulse pounding. Her eyelids fluttered closed.

She felt a chaste peck on her forehead. Startled, she opened her eyes. He dropped his hand and pulled back. "It's late," he said gruffly. "I think we'd better call it a night before we do something we'll both regret. You take the bedroom. I'll sleep out here."

He rose from his chair as she'd seen him do a thousand times, in that decisive way that signalled a meeting was over. His eyes were once more shuttered, his expression again impassive.

Kate scrambled to her feet and pulled herself to her most erect posture, struggling to act composed. She gave a stiff nod. "I—I guess I'll see you in the morning."

"Okay. Good night." He turned away and stared out the window, seemingly absorbed in the nighttime view of the French Quarter.

She hurried to the bedroom and closed the door behind her, her heart beating fast and hard, her emotions in turmoil.

He was right, she told herself. The kiss at the altar had been for the benefit of Birdie and the other guests. A kiss in private would be an entirely different matter.

But he'd very nearly kissed her again. The thought made her stomach quiver like a violin string stroked by a bow.

She sank to the bed and tried to reason with her heart, which felt as if it might bound out of her chest at any moment. The marriage was nothing but a business arrangement, she told herself sternly.

But something distinctly unbusinesslike was going on between them, something that had begun with that kiss at the altar and grown during their conversation tonight.

Richard was attracted to her. Excitement raced up her spine, and an illicit thrill curled like a wave in her chest.

It didn't mean anything, she told herself sternly. Richard was attracted to lots of women. He wasn't interested in commitment or marriage. There was no possibility of a future with him. It would be professionally disastrous to get romantically involved with her boss.

Richard was attracted to her, her heart hummed loudly.

Well, so what? her mind argued. *That doesn't change anything.*

Yes, it does, her heart responded. *It changes everything.*

"You're being ridiculous," she whispered to herself. The champagne and the circumstances and the late hour had combined to create a dangerously seductive situation, that was all. Their relationship would be back to normal in the morning.

But deep inside, Kate was certain it would never be the same again.

Chapter Five

"**Y**ou can't be serious." Richard stared at Birdie, certain the old bat had fallen out of her belfry.

Birdie leaned across her gilt-edged desk. "I'm perfectly serious. Louie and I always lived at the hotel, and I expect the new owners to do the same. It's a very common practice for hoteliers, you know."

"It's equally common for them to have their own homes elsewhere. I happen to have a perfectly fine home in the Garden District, and that's where Kate and I intend to reside." He glanced at Kate, who was seated beside him on the love seat in Birdie's office. Her complexion had gone ashen, he noted—a hard thing to do in a room where every light socket held a pink bulb.

No telling what color his own face was—blue from suppressed curses, most likely. He'd had all of the meddling he intended to take from the overbearing Birdie Delacroix. Not only was it her fault he was now a married man, it was also her fault he'd spent a tormenting night on a sofa that was way too short for his legs.

He preferred to blame his sleeplessness on Birdie and the

uncomfortable couch than on the uneasy sense of guilt that had gnawed at his gut all night. He had no business exploiting Kate's innate kindness for his own purposes—and he'd had even less business entertaining the exquisitely inappropriate thoughts of her that had taunted all him night long. Hell, he'd almost kissed her again last night, even after finding out about her dreams and values.

He was the lowest type of cad. His only saving grace was that he'd stopped himself at the very last moment.

He'd finally fallen asleep at dawn, only to awaken with a splitting headache and the grim realization that Kate looked even sexier in jeans and a T-shirt than she had in that form-hugging dress.

Dammit, there was no reason that going through with that ridiculous ceremony yesterday should make him feel so different around her, but it had. Instead of being comfortable and at ease, he felt awkward and self-conscious and unsure how to treat her.

She was no longer just his secretary. She was his wife. He'd known they were going to get married, but he hadn't expected to *feel* married.

Work—that was what he needed to focus on. Things between himself and Kate would get back to normal once they started working together again. It was Sunday, but he'd never differentiated much between workdays and weekends. He had a key to the office and was anxious to get started. He'd told Birdie he wanted the thirty-day trial period to begin immediately, and he wanted to settle into his new office as soon as possible. Kate was going to take over the old woman's pink office, and Richard would move into the larger adjoining one previously occupied by Louie.

Kate had seemed as eager to vacate their bogus love nest as he was. So, after a quick room service breakfast, they'd headed down to the administrative offices on the first floor and found Birdie clearing out her desk.

She'd subjected them to a sly inquiry about how well they'd

slept, then dropped her bombshell. "I bet you two are ready to see your new quarters," she'd perkily announced.

"New quarters?" they'd echoed simultaneously, looking at each other.

Birdie's painted eyebrows had flown high on her forehead in an unconvincing display of dismay. "Oh, dear. Have I forgotten to mention that you have living quarters here at the hotel?"

Forgotten, my assets, Richard had thought grimly.

"It's an incredibly convenient arrangement," the flamboyant old dowager said now, adjusting the voluminous sleeves of what looked like a pink muumuu.

"Convenience isn't the issue. Kate and I are newlyweds, and we want our privacy." Richard reached his arm around Kate for emphasis. The skin of her upper arm was warm, almost feverish, yet he felt goose bumps rise under his fingers.

Was his touch doing that to her? The thought gave him goose bumps of his own. He ran his hand up and down her arm, tantalized by the texture of her skin.

"You'll have plenty of privacy here. Just think—you can have private lunches and afternoon tête-à-têtes and who knows what else in your quarters whenever you feel the need for a private...ah, conference." She batted her improbably long eyelashes suggestively.

The last thing he needed was additional suggestions about what to do in private with Kate. Richard's fingers tensed on Kate's arm. "I'm afraid it's completely out of the question. Kate and I have been looking forward to making a home together. I'm sure you can understand."

"Of course," Birdie said amiably. "And after this little trial period is over and the hotel is completely yours, why, you can live anywhere you want."

Richard narrowed his eyes. "If that's the case, why can't we go ahead and live where we want right now?"

Birdie fixed him with a patient smile. "Because of the employees, Richard, dear. It will be so much easier for them to get used to you if you're here full time, at least in the beginning—especially since I'll still be living here. I want them to start coming to *you* with their questions and problems, not me." She pursed her lips. "I know this is a bit of an imposition, but I promised my Louie I'd sell the hotel only to a couple who would put the needs of the employees before their own, and I'm certain you have the best interests of the employees at heart. It isn't really such a terrible inconvenience, is it, my dears?"

She was the most manipulative, interfering, bossy old dame Richard had ever had the displeasure of doing business with, and he'd had all he intended to take. He leaned forward and scowled. "It damn sure—"

"Is something we'll need to discuss, right, honey?" Kate interrupted, her hand on his arm. She turned to Birdie with a smile. "Would you mind if we took a few minutes to talk it over?"

"Of course not. Go look at your living quarters while you talk." She opened her drawer, pulled out a massive key ring and took off a key, then held it out to Richard. "You may remember it. It's the suite on the third floor with the little kitchen."

Richard turned to Kate as the elevator door slid closed behind them a few moments later. "I had no idea she was going to spring this on us."

Kate gave a dry smile, fixing her eyes on the numbers above the door. "Really? I never would have known."

He was not to be cajoled out of his black mood. "I suppose I should thank you for keeping me from strangling her," he said grudgingly. "But I won't allow her to manipulate us like this."

"Birdie seems pretty determined to have her way." Kate sneaked a glance at him from the corner of her eye. His mouth was set in the hard, firm line that usually meant his mind was made up.

"Well, so am I." He raked his hand through his hair, then jammed it in the pocket of his khaki slacks. "I've already taken advantage of your good nature by talking you into marrying me. I refuse to ask you to actually live with me, too. You've already gone way beyond the call of duty.''

He was concerned about her—that was why he was so upset. The thought made her pulse quicken. ''But—but you'll lose the hotel.''

''Nah. The old dame's bluffing.''

''I don't think so.''

''No?'' Richard leveled a serious gaze at her. ''Why not?''

A little jolt of pleasure shot through her at the weight Richard seemed to give her opinion. At her previous job, her boss had treated her as if she were nothing but a set of clerical skills. Richard, on the other hand, often sought her input and always seemed to value it. It was one of the things she loved most about her job—the feeling that she was a contributing partner, not just a mere employee.

She sought to phrase her thoughts in a way deserving of such consideration. ''Well, for one thing, Birdie's determined to keep her promise to her husband. For another, she genuinely thinks of the employees as family. I'm afraid that if she questions your commitment to their well-being, she'll look for another buyer.''

Richard studied her face, his expression thoughtful. ''Surely she wouldn't renege on the deal now. Not after all the trouble she went to arranging our wedding.''

''Birdie didn't think of it as trouble,'' she replied. ''She had a ball. Besides, she might be softhearted and sentimental, but underneath it all, I suspect she's tough as nails. She'll do whatever she thinks she has to do to protect the best interests of this hotel.''

The elevator door abruptly slid open. A couple stood in the foyer, blocking the elevator exit, so involved in a passionate kiss that they were oblivious to Kate and Richard's arrival. Richard diplomatically cleared his throat.

Startled and embarrassed, the pair jumped apart, making space for Kate and Richard to disembark. The red-faced young man grabbed the woman's hand and pulled her into the elevator with him. "We, uh, were just married yesterday," he explained sheepishly, just before the door slid closed.

So were we. Kate glanced at Richard, and the uneasy expression on his face told her his thoughts mirrored her own. He cleared his throat again. "I guess that sort of thing is bound to happen in a place called the Honeymoon Hotel."

"I guess so." Kate walked in awkward silence beside him down the plushly carpeted hallway, strangely depressed. There was quite a contrast between the lovestruck couple's passionate behavior and the awkward stiltedness between her and Richard. That was the way newlyweds were supposed to act when they were alone together, she thought—affectionate and warm and loving, not tense and rigid and cautious.

Of course, she reminded herself, she and Richard weren't really married, not in the in-love, committed-for-all-time way the other couple was. Still, it seemed as if things had become unnaturally strained between them ever since the minister had proclaimed them husband and wife. Was it just the fact that they were married, or was it the result of that kiss?

She didn't know. She only knew she was afraid to get too close to him, afraid that the slightest touch would set off a thought-fogging physical reaction, afraid that she would act in some embarrassingly inappropriate, unprofessional manner that would let him know how very much she wanted him to kiss her in private the way he'd kissed in front of the congregation.

The memory made her heart race. She was relieved when Richard stopped outside a door at the end of the hall.

"Here we are." He inserted the key in the doorknob, turned it and swung the door open.

Kate stepped into a living room that was smaller and less elaborately furnished than last night's suite, but tastefully decorated all the same in soft tones of blue and rose and green. A bedroom with a queen-size bed and bathroom were situated to the left through a doorway. At the far end was a dining area, flanked by a small kitchen and a half bath.

"It's lovely," Kate murmured.

Richard gave the room a cursory glance, then stalked to the window. He stared out, his eyes narrowed. "Maybe Birdie will accept a compromise. If we promise to arrive at the hotel at, say, six each morning and not leave until eight in the evening, maybe she won't insist on us living here."

Kate's fingers drifted across the back of the floral sofa as she crossed the room. "I don't think that will address the real reason she wants us to stay."

"What do you mean?"

Kate hesitated, trying to think of a way to logically explain the emotional reason, as she knew Richard discounted anything that wasn't based on hard, cold facts. "Home is where the heart is, and this hotel has been Birdie's home for nearly half a century. She's finding it hard to cut loose of something she's so attached to. I think she subconsciously needs to see us making the hotel our home, getting really attached to it ourselves, so she can let the place go."

Richard gazed at her for a long moment. "You're scaring me, Kate."

"Scaring you?"

"Yeah. What you just said has no basis in sound business practice, but it actually seemed to make sense."

Kate couldn't repress a grin. "What's so scary about that?"

"I happen to find it pretty terrifying that my wife is on the same wavelength as that ditzy old dame."

My wife. The words left her breathless and weak-limbed with a racing pulse as if she'd just finished a lengthy jog.

She stared at him. From the way he stared back, she gathered that he, too, was surprised at what he'd just said. Sounds of the French Quarter drifted through the window—the plaintive wail of a street musician's saxophone, a woman's laugh, the rumble of a truck, the deep bleat of a distant foghorn on the river. But a disquieting silence filled the room.

Richard shoved his hands in his pockets and looked away. "The fact that you're starting to make the workings of that old gal's mind seem understandable to me is a pretty spooky concept, too." He turned his back to her to again gaze out the window. "There's got to be a solution to this dilemma."

She had one. She simply had to find the nerve to voice it. "Maybe it's not as difficult as you think," she finally ventured.

"What do you mean?"

"It's just for a month. Why don't we simply do what she wants?" Oh, dear heavens—what was she saying? What was she thinking? She didn't know. She only knew she had a sudden, desperate, compelling urge to seize this opportunity before it slipped away.

Opportunity? Opportunity for what?

Her heart was drumming like a percussion instrument, so hard and so loud she feared he could hear it. Richard was looking at her strangely. She didn't want him to know how rattled she felt. She wanted to act nonchalant, as if she thought living with him was no big deal.

"We've already jumped off the deep end by getting married. It would be a shame to have gone to all this trouble only to give up now."

"I didn't say I wanted to give up," he said quickly.

That made two of them. He didn't want to lose his chance to win the hotel, and she didn't want to lose her chance to win him.

Win him? The thought alarmed her. Was that what she was hoping to do?

No. Of course not. It was just a wild, random thought. Annie had no doubt planted the suggestion with all her nonsensical talk yesterday.

She gave what she hoped was a casual shrug. "We're both adults, after all. I'm sure we'll be able to control ourselves around each other."

Richard didn't share her confidence. The thought of living in such close proximity to Kate for four weeks made his throat feel like the Sahara.

"I'm not so sure about that." The rejoinder lacked the comedic tone he'd aimed for, but he wasn't feeling any too witty at the moment. He was feeling panic-stricken.

What was the matter with him? Kate was handing him a lifeline, and instead of grabbing it with both hands, he was debating whether to take it or not.

He was becoming as irrational as Birdie, he thought with self-disgust. What the heck was he so worried about? The prospect of sharing an apartment didn't seem to be causing Kate any great anxiety. From her unconcerned tone and demeanor, it looked as if the concept excited her as much as the prospect of watching grass grow.

He needed to get a grip on himself, he thought sternly. After all, as she'd just said, they were both adults. If she was comfortable with the situation, he'd be a fool to pass up the offer.

"I really appreciate this, Kate." He reached out and took her hands, and the moment his skin made contact with hers, he knew he'd made a tactical error. The feel of her skin changed things—his ability to think, the temperature of the room, the speed at which the blood flowed in his veins.

His eyes fastened on her lips. They were slightly parted, plump and tempting as summer peaches. He was dying to pull her close, lower his head and claim her inviting mouth. He remembered the texture of her lips, the hot, sweet taste of her mouth.

He abruptly dropped her hands and stepped back. No. He couldn't kiss her, he couldn't even touch her when they were alone. That was the key to making this whole thing work. If he didn't touch her, he couldn't get carried away, couldn't lose his head, couldn't do something he would surely regret.

Because he would surely regret it if he took advantage of Kate under the circumstances.

"Come on," he said, in a voice that sounded lower and rougher than usual. "Let's go tell the old biddy she's won another round."

Annie looked around the small suite. "You've been living here for a whole week with the sexiest man in New Orleans—

excepting my Steve, of course—and nothing's happened?''
She eyed Kate incredulously over her half-eaten plate of tuna
salad. ''Nothing at all?''

''Nothing. I swear it. Would you like some more iced tea?''
Kate rose from the dining table to retrieve a pitcher from the
kitchen. Her friend had come by for lunch, and Kate had decided to prepare it in her suite instead of taking Anne to the
hotel restaurant. It had been a wise decision, Kate thought,
refilling her friend's glass. Annie was full of questions she
wouldn't have wanted any hotel employees to overhear.

''Not even a little kiss?''

''No.'' Kate set the pitcher on the kitchen counter and returned to the table.

''How about a good-night peck on the cheek?''

''I'm usually in bed before he even comes upstairs from the
office,'' Kate admitted.

''And?''

''And nothing. I never see him. He sleeps on the sofa in
the living room, and I sleep in the bedroom.''

''Well, he must come through the bedroom to use the
shower.''

Kate shook her head. ''He showers in the hotel's health club
after he runs and works out each morning.''

Annie curiously eyed the couch at the far end of the room.
''What does he sleep in?''

''I have no idea.''

Annie placed a hand on her hip and frowned at her friend.
''Are you putting me on?''

Kate shrugged. ''He's up at the crack of dawn. I wait until
he leaves before I come out of the bedroom.''

Annie stared at her in amazement. ''This defies the laws of
nature. You realize that, don't you?''

Oh, she realized it, all right. Her nerves were frayed and
her mind was frazzled from the stress of it all. It was pure
torture, but it was torture of her own making. After all, she'd
been the one who'd insisted they go along with Birdie's plan.

She sighed. "It's not a real marriage, Annie. We knew that from the outset."

"But you two are living together. How can you live with someone and never see him?"

"I do see him. At work."

"Oh, excuse me." Annie rolled her eyes. "And how are things at work?"

"Polite."

"Polite? What the heck does that mean?"

Kate slumped back in her chair and sighed. "He's—restrained. Proper. Stuffy, even. He never kids around or asks my opinion about things anymore. When Birdie's around, he calls me 'sweetheart,' but that's it."

"Surely you two talk during meals."

Kate shook her head. "He eats breakfast, lunch and dinner in meetings—he's at a luncheon right now. Failing that, he has room service send meals to his office."

"Wow. Sounds like getting married really ruined your relationship."

It was true, Kate thought woefully. They used to tease and banter and eat lunch together as a matter of course. Now Richard silently handed her stacks of work, treated her with stiff formality when she took notes at meetings and seldom said more than "thank you" when she brought him phone messages and correspondence. She missed the camaraderie, the easy sense of rapport, the feeling that she was an important part of his team. She was beginning to feel like a faceless employee, an interchangeable cog in the hotel's administrative wheel.

She sure didn't feel like a wife, she thought glumly.

"Birdie's a pretty sharp lady," Annie remarked. "She must be getting suspicious."

"I'm afraid she is," Kate admitted. "She told me yesterday that in a good marriage, the couple works as partners. She said she wants me to get more involved in the hotel, to take on some projects of my own and let the secretarial staff handle more of Richard's clerical work."

"What did Richard say?"

"'Fine.' He didn't seem to care. Sometimes I think I've become invisible to him."

Annie laughed. "My guess is it's just the opposite."

"Well, I think he sees this as a small, easy-to-make concession to Birdie. After the way she meddled in our personal life, I think he expected her to be peering over his shoulder and second-guessing his every move, but she's actually stepped aside to let him run the hotel. This is the first operational suggestion she's made."

"So what's your project going to be?"

"Public relations. Richard thinks we need to try to book more local business in the ballroom and banquet rooms, so I'm going to try to increase the hotel's involvement in the community."

"How are you going to do that?"

"I don't know yet."

Annie checked her watch, then drained her tea glass and scooted back her chair. "I hate to say it, but I've got to get back to work."

Kate walked her to the door. Annie gave her a hug, then picked up her purse from a side table and paused, her hand on the doorknob. "While you're working on that public relations plan of yours, you'd better dream up a *private* relations plan as well."

"What do you mean?"

"You and Richard wouldn't be going to this much trouble to avoid each other if there wasn't something to avoid. Something's going on between you two. I saw it when he kissed you at the wedding, and I don't buy your theory that he was faking it. Nobody could fake a kiss like that."

"You're as full of romantic notions as Birdie. Richard wants to keep things platonic as much as I do."

"Which isn't much at all." Annie laughed, slung her purse on her shoulder and gave Kate a knowing look. "You don't have to take my word for it. If you want to find out how he really feels about you, just figure out a way to get him to kiss you again.''

"Have you figured it out yet?" Richard asked later that afternoon.

Startled, Kate sat bolt upright at her desk. "Figured out what?"

"Your first public relations project. Birdie's been bugging me about it."

"Oh." Kate ran a hand self-consciously through her hair. She'd been so preoccupied with Annie's earlier remark that she hadn't noticed him enter her office through his adjoining door. For a split second, she'd been afraid he'd added mind reading to the growing list of ways he was getting under her skin.

Because he definitely was. Ever since she'd gotten that glimpse into his childhood and his reasons for wanting the hotel, a most unprofessional tenderness toward him had developed. That kiss at the wedding hadn't helped matters. Neither did the fact that he was sleeping in the next room, or that the employees called her by his last name. The fantasies she'd entertained about him for months had picked up strength and velocity like a hurricane at sea. She used to be able to more or less put her secret crush on Richard on hold during the workday, but it was getting harder and harder to do so. Distinctly unbusinesslike thoughts had started cropping up at the most inappropriate moments.

Right now, for example. Kate straightened her jacket, hoping she looked a lot more composed than she felt. "As a matter of fact, I've not only figured it out, but I've set it in motion."

"Oh, really?" Richard seated himself on the edge of the desk and smiled. It was his old smile—warm and interested and intensely focused—and it affected her like a heat lamp. "When do I get to hear about it?"

"Tonight. Over dinner."

The moment she said it, she realized how suggestive it

sounded—as if she were planning an intimate candlelit supper. She couldn't deny that the thought had crossed her mind. She'd dismissed it immediately, reminding herself of all the reasons Richard was a poor romantic risk, telling herself he wouldn't be interested, anyway.

Or would he? Was it possible that Annie was right—that Richard *was* attracted to her, that he was avoiding her out of some misguided notion of chivalry?

She sneaked a sideways glance at his face and caught him studying her intently, his mouth curved in a smile. Her heart jumped like a jackrabbit, and she quickly looked away.

Her imagination was working overtime again, that was all, she told herself sternly. And even if it wasn't, the last thing she needed to do was get involved with a confirmed bachelor.

Darn that Annie—she had a way of making Kate lose sight of reality. The cold, stark fact was that Richard was completely opposed to marriage, and Kate would be happy with nothing less.

But Richard is already married to you, piped up a traitorous little voice inside her head. *All you have to do is make him like it.*

The thought made her face warm. So did the way Richard's eyes met hers, and the husky note in his voice. "Are you inviting me to dinner?"

"Along with some other guests," she quickly replied.

Was it wishful thinking, or did he actually look disappointed for one fleeting second? she wondered as she watched him rub his jaw.

"Members of the media?" he asked. "That's probably a good idea, getting to know some of the local journalists."

"That's not who I invited. Although channel seven is coming to cover it for the evening news."

Richard frowned in consternation. "What are you talking about?"

Kate drew a deep breath and plunged in. "Well, Annie came for lunch, and after she left, I flipped on the TV while I cleaned up the kitchen. Channel seven was running a story about this local family, the Winfields, whose home had burned down. They have two young children and a brand-new baby. Everyone got out safely, but all of their possessions were destroyed.''

"Wow, that's rough.'' Richard shook his head sympathetically. "But I don't see what that has to do with us. People have homeowner's insurance for that kind of thing.''

Kate twisted her fingers together in her lap, suddenly wishing she'd gotten Richard's approval before she'd proceeded. But Richard had told her to handle the hotel's public relations on her own, and when she'd learn of the Winfields' plight and realized she had it within her power to help them, she'd just been unable to resist.

"They didn't have homeowner's insurance because they were renting their home. They don't have much money, either,'' Kate explained. "The husband is a car mechanic, but he got laid off last year and was unemployed for a long time. He has a job now, but the long stretch of unemployment ate up all their savings. They have no family and nowhere to go.''

Kate drew a deep breath and finished in a rush. "So I called the station, talked to the reporter who'd done the story and offered to let the family stay here until they can get back on their feet.''

"You what?''

"Offered to let them stay here.''

Alarm surged through Richard. "Starting when?''

"Tonight.''

Richard placed both hands on her desk and leaned forward. "Kate, did you look at the occupancy report? We're sold out for the next two nights. This is the first time in two years that this hotel stands to make a profit. It's my chance to prove to Birdie that I can make a go of this place. I've spent the past week meeting with the larger convention hotels, convincing them to let us take their overflow business, and this is our test run. I promised a block of seventy-five rooms, and by golly, that's what I intend to deliver.''

"Well, then, the family can stay with us.''

"In our suite?" He stared at her incredulously. "That's going to be a little crowded, don't you think?" Hell, it was already way too crowded with just the two of them.

"I've got a better idea," chimed in a familiar voice from the doorway. "You two can stay with me."

Great, Richard thought grimly; just what this situation needed to slide from problematic to dire without passing Go—interference from the Birdmeister. He turned toward his pink-clad nemesis and raised a questioning eyebrow. "Stay with you?"

"Why, yes. My apartment has two bedrooms. You can let that poor family take your suite where they'll have plenty of room, and you two can stay with me."

Richard forced a smile. "That's not necessary. Kate didn't understand the situation earlier. Now that she does, I'm sure she'll agree that we need to postpone the invitation until next week."

One look at Kate's furrowed brow and compressed lips told him otherwise. "They need a place to stay now, not next week."

Blast. Whose side was she on, anyway? Richard jammed his hands in his pockets. "There are shelters for this sort of thing."

Kate's chin tilted up. "There's also my apartment. The hotel won't get any publicity that way, but at least that newborn baby will have a safe, clean place to stay."

"You still have an apartment?" Birdie advanced on Kate, her brow drawn, her eyes narrowed. Her voice held a suspicious note that made Richard's blood run cold. "What on earth for, dear?"

Richard suppressed a groan. Trust Birdie to pick up on the slightest slip. He glanced at Kate as her eyes sought his, worried and alarmed and apologetic. He took a protective step toward her, thinking fast. "Her, uh, lease isn't up yet."

Birdie looked only partially placated. Richard silently swore. The last thing he wanted was for the old woman to grow more suspicious about the state of his marriage than she already was. Just this morning she'd made a worrisome remark about the number of hours he was spending in the office. "I appreciate all your hard work, Richard, but don't neglect your wife," she'd said, her light tone belied by the serious look in her eye. "Newlyweds need to spend time together doing things besides working. No matter how good you are at running the hotel, I can't sell it to you if your marriage isn't happy."

He needed to divert the old woman from any further speculation on his relationship with Kate, and he needed to do it fast. His best bet was to direct her thoughts to the hotel.

"The next couple of days are crucial to this hotel's long-term success," he explained. "If we handle this group well, we have the potential of filling the hotel on a regular basis in the future. As a businesswoman, I'm sure you can see that providing the promised number of rooms is a lot more important than giving a handout to a family that any number of social service agencies can help more efficiently."

"Depends on your definition of important." Birdie peered over her glasses in displeasure. "But that's beside the point. Your wife has issued an invitation, and you must support her." She turned to Kate, and her expression, along with her tone, softened. "Luckily, we can achieve both goals. I'll send a maid to move some of your things to my spare room and get your suite ready for this family to occupy."

"Richard and I don't want to put you to any trouble. We can go stay at Richard's place—I mean, *our* place—until the Winfields leave."

"Nonsense, dear, it's no trouble at all. I'll enjoy having you as my guests. In fact, I insist on it." Without giving them the opportunity to protest further, the old woman swept from the room.

Kate turned to Richard, her expression apologetic. "I didn't mean to mention my apartment. Sorry."

"That's the least of my worries." There were more immediate concerns to deal with, he thought grimly—such as the fact that he and Kate were going to be sharing a bedroom for the next two nights. The thought made him swallow hard.

He could manage the hotel, he could correct its financial problems, he could even put up with Birdie—but he didn't have a clue how to cope with Kate. She was wreaking havoc with his hormones. Just when he needed to be focusing on business strategies, his mind would veer to his wife.

His wife. Now why on earth did he keep thinking about her in those terms, when he knew darn well the marriage was only a farce?

And how had he managed to work with her for eight months and not notice how attractive she was? He must have been blind. But now that his eyes were opened, he couldn't look at her without noticing the delicate curve of her cheek, the dark sweep of lashes above her green eyes, the lush fullness of her lips. It was annoying as hell.

He'd hoped that once they started working together again, things would settle back to normal, but they hadn't. He'd tried staying out of her way, tried limiting his contact with her, tried treating her strictly as an employee, but those tactics hadn't worked, either.

Distancing himself from her had only made him miss her. A dozen times a day he was tempted to call her in or drop by her desk to ask her opinion about something. He hadn't realized how heavily he'd grown to rely on her judgment, how accustomed he'd become to bouncing ideas off her.

It was downright scary, how much of his mental energy she was consuming.

Richard heaved a sigh. This whole phony marriage was a lot more complex than he'd ever imagined—and not for any of the reasons he would have thought. Now that Birdie was acting suspicious, he was going to have to put more effort into acting like a newlywed—and for the next two nights, at least, he was going to have to do it under the eagle-eyed old bird's constant scrutiny.

Richard rubbed the back of his neck, where a tension headache coiled like a snake. How was he going to manage to share a bedroom with Kate without losing his mind—or, even worse, his resolve to keep their relationship strictly platonic?

Chapter Six

Mrs. Winfield smiled down at the four-year-old girl clinging to her elbow and adjusted the sleeping newborn in her arms. "Dinner was wonderful," she said to Kate and Richard, as she and her husband accompanied them out of the hotel restaurant and into the lobby. "Thank you so much for a lovely meal."

"And for giving us a roof over our heads," added Mr. Winfield, shifting a drowsy two-year-old to his left arm and extending his right hand to Richard. "If it weren't for you, we'd be bunking in two or three separate public shelters this weekend. It means a lot to us to get to stay together, especially at a time like this." His eyes glimmered suspiciously. For a moment, Richard was afraid the tall, husky man was going to cry. "Thank you," he added thickly.

Richard felt a lump form in his own throat as he shook the man's hand. "It's our pleasure. But Kate here deserves all the credit."

To put it mildly, he thought guiltily. If he'd had his way, the family *would* be spread out all over town. He was grateful Kate had insisted that they stay here.

Richard watched her talk with the Winfields, downplaying her role in providing their accommodations. She'd told him she'd issued the invitation as part of a public relations plan, and it was true that the local TV station had shot a follow-up feature about the hotel's generosity, but Richard was certain that publicity had not been Kate's motivating concern.

She had a heart as soft as warm taffy. The thought simultaneously touched him and sent an irrational surge of irritation washing over him. He'd never met anyone as considerate, as compassionate, as kind as Kate. How could he be annoyed at her for having such a generous spirit? He didn't know, but he was aggravated all the same.

But not at Kate. At himself. He was angry that he was so drawn to her, annoyed that he'd put her in this compromising position and irked that he wanted nothing more than to compromise her further.

Dammit, he didn't need this sort of distraction right now. He didn't need anyone or anything diverting him from his goal of convincing Birdie to sell him the property so he could turn it into a business hotel.

His thoughts were jerked back to the present by a sharp tug on the bottom of his jacket. "Can I go to bed now, mister?"

Nonplussed, Richard glanced over at Kate, who reached down and fluffed the young girl's downy blond hair. "Of course you can, honey. We've got two roll-away beds set up in the living room of the suite for you and your sister, and a crib in the bedroom for your baby brother."

"I don't know how to thank you," Mrs. Winfield repeated.

"We're just glad we can be of assistance," Kate replied. "Why don't you head on upstairs? You've had a long day."

After another round of thank-yous, the Winfields boarded an elevator vacated by a gray-headed bellman wheeling an empty luggage cart. The bellman tipped the bill of his scarlet cap and flashed a row of gleaming dentures. "'Evening, Mr. Chandler, Mrs. Chandler."

"Good evening, Charles," Kate responded.

Richard glanced at her sharply. Trust Kate to know the

man's name, he thought wryly. She'd probably memorized the entire payroll list.

"Mighty nice, what you folks are doing for that family," Charles said. "I saw it on the evening news in the break room, and I sure was impressed."

"You have Mrs. Chandler here to thank for that," Richard said gruffly.

"Well, it's mighty nice. Makes me proud to work for the Honeymoon Hotel. The rest of the employees were sayin' so, too." Charles lumbered toward the hotel entrance with the cart.

Good grief, she was simply too good to be true. He wished he could find a flaw to hold against Kate as a shield from the unwanted affection he was developing toward her, but none came to mind.

And now he had to say something gracious. Simple decency demanded it.

"He's right, you know. It is mighty nice," he finally managed.

Kate's expression of pleasure warmed him straight through. "They're a lovely family, aren't they?"

"Yes." But the family wasn't what Richard was thinking was lovely at the moment. It was Kate. Her hair shone with copper highlights in the lobby chandelier, and her green eyes looked as soft and inviting as a field of clover. It wasn't just her appearance he was attracted to, he realized suddenly. It was *her*—her warmth, her kindness, her giving nature.

Alarm shot through him, making his palms cold and clammy.

"The Winfields remind me of my parents," she continued. "Did you see the way they looked at each other during dinner? And I was touched by the way they kept trying to give each other credit for getting the family safely out of the house during the fire."

"It was pretty unusual," Richard said tightly. "In most marriages, the husband and wife would be arguing over whose fault it was that they don't have any money or resources."

Kate's gaze rested warmly on him. "It must have been hard on you, growing up with parents who didn't get along."

He hadn't said a word about his family. But he hadn't needed to, he realized. He'd evidently said enough earlier. He gave an offhand shrug. "It left me with a healthy cynicism, that's all."

"You think cynicism's healthy?"

"Healthier than a Pollyanna approach," he said defensively. "A person who's cynical won't be blindsided by the realities of life."

"But a lot of realities are good. Cynics miss some of the best things in life because they're too busy looking for problems."

"Maybe it's better not to see what you can't have."

"You mean a marriage like the Winfields'?"

Richard lifted his shoulders noncommitally and pretended to examine the flower arrangement on the lobby table. "Not everyone's cut out for happily ever after. People who didn't grow up in happy homes have poor odds of ever creating one for themselves."

He felt the disconcerting weight of her hand on his arm. "They can if they're willing to try. I don't think it's ever too late to learn something you really want to learn."

What he really wanted to learn was the texture of her skin, the feel of her hair, the places she applied the perfume that was weaving a soft, intoxicating spell around him. He wanted to know if she felt as warm on the inside as she seemed, if all of her was as sweet as her lips, if she was as giving in bed as she was everywhere else. He longed to pull her into his arms and claim her mouth, to take her upstairs and undress her and make excruciatingly slow love to her until they were both begging and panting.

A surge of panic washed over him. He couldn't let her have this effect on him. She made him feel understood and cared about, and he didn't want to feel that way. He didn't want to feel, period. He wanted to remain detached, indifferent, uninvolved.

Most of all, he didn't want to feel that he was personally letting her down when she discovered, as she ultimately would, that his long-term intention wasn't to operate the hotel but to renovate and sell it.

Better for her to think he was a jerk now than later. "The fact of the matter is, I'm not interested in marriage at all, except as a way of the getting this hotel." That much, at least, was the truth. He jabbed the elevator button and was glad when one arrived almost immediately. "Let's head up. I'm positive Birdie's waiting."

Sure enough, she was. The elderly woman answered the door before they'd even finished knocking, wearing an enormous smile and an even more enormous rose caftan. "Welcome, my dears! Come right on in."

She threw open the door, and Kate stepped into an apartment that appeared to be a cross between Ali Baba's cave and a Victorian parlor. Elaborate pillows, Persian rugs, heavy fringed drapes and a wild mixture of prints and patterns created a dizzying scheme of colors and textures.

"The guest room is over this way." She led them across the living area to a tiny hallway, then flung open a door.

The bedroom was small—almost claustrophobically so. It featured a gleaming hardwood floor and a large four-poster bed that seemed to expand as Kate stared at it. The crimson damask comforter was turned down to expose creamy, lace-edged sheets. Plump, inviting pillows nestled against the headboard.

"You've got your own bathroom here," Birdie chirped, flipping on a light in a closet-size room. "As you can see, a maid brought up all your toiletry items and arranged them for you." She opened an old-fashioned pull drawer in the wall. "This is the laundry chute. Just drop your dirty clothes in here, and they'll go straight to the hotel laundry in the basement."

"Where are our clothes and other things?" Richard asked.

"In the closet. The only thing I told the maid not to bother with was your nightclothes."

"We don't have any nightclothes?" Kate asked in alarm.

Birdie chortled. "I don't imagine you two newlyweds have much use for them anyway, but I couldn't resist giving you a little gift, Kate, dear. You'll find it in that box on the bed." The old woman gave an elaborate yawn. "Well, if you'll excuse me, I believe I'll retire for the night. If you need anything, my room is right next door."

With a coy smile, she bustled out of the room. Kate stared at Richard, her heart pounding. It was one thing to share close quarters. It was another to share an actual bed. Richard's gaze shifted away, but not before she'd read a message of acute discomfort in his eyes.

She couldn't stand to see him look so miserable. It was up to her to put him at ease. Courage—that's what this situation called for. She needed to act breezy and sophisticated, completely unbothered by the unexpected intimacy. Richard was a man of the world, after all, accustomed to women who were the same way.

"Well, if you don't mind, I guess I'll shower first."

Richard's eyes registered mild surprise. "Fine. Go right ahead."

Kate plucked the box from the middle of the cushy bed and casually sauntered into the bathroom, closing the door behind her.

Once inside, her courage faltered. The thought of taking off her clothes when Richard was just on the other side of the door made her stomach quiver.

She was being ridiculous, she told herself, deliberately peeling off her clothes and dropping them one by one into the laundry chute. He didn't have X-ray vision, for heaven's sake. Besides, she didn't have any solid reason to think he'd be interested in looking at her even if he did.

All the same, Kate hurried through her shower, then rapidly dried off on an enormous pink towel sporting Birdie's initials. Wrapping it around herself, she turned to the steamed-up mirror. She fussed with her hair, then automatically reached for her makeup, which the maid had arranged on the bathroom counter.

Her hand froze on a tube of mascara. What was she thinking? She couldn't show up for bed wearing eye makeup. She wanted to appear confident, soignée and sophisticated—not deliberately seductive.

She settled for biting her lips and pinching her cheeks to give them some color, then picked up Birdie's box. It was large—large enough to hold a winter coat. Knowing Birdie, Kate thought with a smile, it probably contained an elaborate, floor-length peignoir better suited for ballroom dancing than sleeping.

Kate lifted the lid. "Oh, dear," she gasped, easing a wisp of a nightie from the nest of tissue. The straps weren't spaghetti—they were angel-hair pasta. And the pink fabric they were attached to was sheerer than Kate's best panty hose.

Maybe it was supposed to be worn under something else. Kate tore through the mounds of tissue paper, desperately searching for the rest of the ensemble.

There was nothing else in the box.

Kate's stomach sank to the vicinity of her kneecaps as she stared at the tiny, transparent scrap. Oh, mercy—she couldn't go out in *that*.

But she had no choice, she thought ruefully. The dress she'd worn into the bathroom was now six floors below.

Reluctantly relinquishing the towel, she pulled the nightie over her head and turned toward the mirror. Her reflection made her wince. She looked more indecent wearing Birdie's gift than she did stark naked.

She grabbed the towel and again wound it tightly around herself, struggling to find an optimistic thought to shore up her flagging sense of bravado. The towel hid far more than a swimsuit did, she told herself bravely. She'd never felt risqué at the beach.

But the beach was a public place, and the bedroom was very private. And the way she felt about Richard made the prospect of parading around draped in a towel and darn little else daunting, to say the least.

Well, one thing was certain—she couldn't stay in the bathroom all night. There was nothing to do about the situation but brazen it out. Clutching the towel as if it were a life-support system, Kate drew a deep breath and opened the bathroom door.

Richard was sitting on the bed, studying an occupancy report. He looked up, rubbed his eyes, then looked again. His eyes bugged and his face blanched.

"Pardon the towel," she said breezily. "Birdie's idea of nightclothes is rather racy."

He stared at her blankly, as if she'd just addressed him in Chinese. "Racy?" he echoed vacantly.

"Very." She giggled gaily, trying to act unfazed by her state of dishabille. "Why, a hankie would give more coverage."

His Adam's apple bobbed visibly.

"I'll try to find something more appropriate to wear while you're in the shower."

He nodded and swallowed again. "Well, I—I'll get out of your way." He darted into the bathroom as if the hounds of hell were after him.

Kate collapsed on the bed, weak-kneed and shaken. When she heard the shower start, she breathed a sigh of relief. She wished she could just crawl under the covers, pull the blanket over her head and not come out until morning.

But Richard would be under those covers with her. The thought sent her sprinting to the closet, flinging off the towel as she went in search of something, anything, to wear.

Before she could even unzip a suitcase, she heard a knock on the door. *Birdie,* she thought, suppressing a groan. She looked around for the towel but didn't see it anywhere. It must have landed between the wall and the bed.

"Yoo-hoo! Katie, dear!"

Not wanting to take the time to try to locate the towel, Kate yanked the sheet off the turned-down bed, wound it around her and padded to the door.

"Yes?" she said, opening it a crack.

"Sorry to disturb you, my dear, but I've run out of my heart medicine. I keep an extra bottle in the medicine cabinet in your bathroom. Would you mind fetching it for me?"

Kate opened the door slightly wider. "Oh—of course not. I'll get it as soon as Richard comes out of the shower."

Birdie chortled. "You're his wife, dear. Surely he won't mind if you go on in now."

Kate's mouth ran dry.

"It's behind the mirror over the sink. The little brown pill bottle on the bottom shelf."

The shower was still going full force. With any luck, she'd be able to get in and out without Richard even knowing she was in the bathroom. "All right," she said reluctantly.

"You're not going to drag that sheet into the bathroom, are you, dear?" Birdie called, peering through the doorway. "You're likely to get it all wet."

"Oh. Of course not."

Nothing like walking in on your boss in the shower, wearing next to nothing yourself, Kate thought glumly. She placed the sheet back on the bed and marched resolutely toward the bathroom.

"That nightgown looks lovely on you, by the way," Birdie called.

Kate forced a smile over her shoulder, knowing her backside was as exposed as a used roll of film. "Thank you. It was very thoughtful of you to give it to me."

A fog of steam assaulted her as she opened the door. Behind the translucent shower curtain, she could make out the shadow of Richard's torso. He was wide-shouldered and trim-hipped, and his biceps bulged as he reached up to wash his hair. The sight made her mouth feel as if it were packed with cotton.

Walking on tiptoe, she gingerly crossed the room, opened the medicine cabinet and found the bottle Birdie had described. Kate grabbed it and started to beat a hasty retreat when the water abruptly choked off. Her air supply seemed to choke off as well. Her heart pounding crazily, Kate bolted toward the door. She'd made it halfway across the bathroom when the shower curtain scraped open.

The next thing she knew, she was gazing at Richard, just the way God had made him.

She felt as though her feet were glued to the tile floor. Her face caught fire. "B-B-Birdie n-n-needs—" Stammering, she held up the bottle, helpless to continue.

Richard didn't move. He just stared at her in the oddest way, his eyes glassy, his lips slightly parted, as if *she* were the one who was naked.

And, oh, dear heavens—for all the coverage the nightie afforded, she might as well be, she realized in horror. As she stood there, paralyzed by mortification, Richard's body responded in a distinctly masculine manner.

The heat searing her cheeks spread into a full-body blush. She fled the room, slipping on the tile as she went, and slammed the door behind her.

"Here," she said breathlessly, thrusting the bottle at Birdie, who was still standing in the hallway outside the partially opened bedroom door.

"Thank you." The elderly woman peered in curiously. Kate pressed firmly on the door. "Well, you two have a nice evening," Birdie called, just before the door closed in her face.

Kate clicked the lock, then collapsed against the door, wondering how on earth she would ever face Richard again.

"I'm sorry I walked in on you," she tried to explain fifteen minutes later when he emerged from the bathroom.

Richard ran a hand through his damp hair, tightened the towel around his waist and ventured a glance at her. She was curled on the bed, bare feet tucked under her, wearing navy knit shorts and an oversize T-shirt that read Happiness Is A Warm Kitten.

Thank heavens she'd changed out of that centerfold costume, he thought grimly. It had taken another ten minutes un-

der a stream of icy water to get his temperature halfway back
in the normal range.

She plucked at a thread in the crimson comforter, avoiding
eye contact. "Birdie was standing in the doorway waiting,"
she tried to explain. "I shouldn't have let her talk me into it,
but I thought I could get in and out of the bathroom without
your seeing me...."

"Kate, you don't need to apologize."

"Yes, but if I hadn't walked in..."

"Don't worry about it."

"But—"

"It's no big deal. We're two normal human beings who
now know what each other looks like without clothes, that's
all."

But that wasn't all they knew, Richard thought ruefully.
From the way his most masculine asset had stood at attention
and saluted, Kate now knew without a doubt that he found her
desirable.

Very desirable.

Painfully desirable.

Stifling an oath, Richard strode to the closet and rummaged
through his duffel bag for a pair of sweatpants. Any man in
the world would have responded the same way, he consoled
himself. The sight of her in that nightie was what dreams were
made of.

He wondered if she were still wearing the flimsy concoction
under her T-shirt. He immediately censored the thought, silently cursing himself for a fool or worse. Thinking about it
when he was going to have to spend the night with her was
like playing with matches in a dynamite factory.

He snatched a pair of gray sweats from his bag and stalked
back to the bathroom, where he closed the door and yanked
them on. He splashed his face with cold water for good measure, then strode back to the tiny bedroom.

There was no TV, no chair, no sofa—just a bureau, a night
table and that enormous bed. It was the only place in the room

to sit. Even worse, Richard thought grimly, it was the only place to sleep.

The sooner this day ended, the better. Besides, with the lights out, he wouldn't be able to look at Kate and keep admiring little things he'd never noticed about her before—the curve of her lower calf, the roundness of her upper arm, the way her hair swung forward and hid her face as she tried to avoid his gaze.

"Well, I guess we'd better call it a night," he said gruffly.

Awkwardness curled around them. "I guess so." Kate slowly rose and began fussing with the covers. She took her time, carefully folding back the comforter, smoothing the sheets, fluffing the pillows, but it wasn't a chore that could be stretched out for long. She looked up, her hand on the readied bed, and met his gaze. The uneasiness between them thickened.

Richard swallowed. "Why don't I just sleep on the floor?"

"Don't be ridiculous. The floor is hardwood, and we don't have any extra blankets." She ran her hand along the sheet, smoothing an invisible wrinkle. "Besides, there's plenty of room here for both of us. Which side do you want?"

She was such a good sport. He was a heel for having these thoughts about her. "It doesn't matter."

"Well, I'll sleep on the left." She scurried into bed and pulled the covers up to her chin. The mattress squeaked noisily.

He sat down on the right half of the mattress, making it screech again, then reached over and flipped off the bedside lamp. The room plunged into darkness.

He carefully stretched out beside her. They weren't touching, but he swore he could feel the heat of her body beside him. His eyes gradually adjusted to the faint light filtering through the partially lowered window shade. He glanced sideways, and saw the outline of her profile.

Don't look at her. Don't think about her. The bed squawked like a seagull as he resolutely rolled on his back and stared at the ceiling.

"Richard?"

"Yes?"

"I didn't mean to embarrass you earlier."

She was embarrassing him all over again by bringing the subject up once more. "You didn't."

"Well, I embarrassed myself." Her voice was thin and reedy. "Not by seeing you," she added quickly, as if she'd just realized how the remark must have sounded. "By you seeing me. I—I was mortified."

"Hey, it's no big deal. The human body is nothing to be ashamed of."

"It is when you're built like me." The remark came out in a muttered rush, like a thought unintentionally spoken aloud. In the flickering light through the window, Richard saw her fling her arm over her eyes, as if she'd just embarrassed herself further.

He was too curious to leave the comment alone. "What do you mean?"

"Nothing. Just that I'm not exactly built like the girls you usually date." Her voice was shaky, and the words seemed to catch in her throat.

"You looked perfectly fine to me." To put it mildly, he thought wryly.

"I can think of a couple of places I'm pretty deficient."

Richard propped up an elbow and stared down at her. "What on earth are you talking about?"

Kate turned her face toward the wall, still shielding her eyes under her arm. "The size of my chest."

"What about it?"

He heard the long, low hiss of her sigh. "I used to get teased about it at school. 'If McCormick turns sideways and sticks out her tongue, she looks like a zipper,' the boys used to say."

"You don't look anything like a zipper to me."

"Well, I've filled out a little since then, but not much. I guess the thing that really made me self-conscious about it is that my former boyfriend…" Her voice trailed off, and for a moment Richard thought she wasn't going to continue. Protectiveness swelled within him, along with a surprising, sudden anger toward this unknown, nameless man who had somehow hurt Kate.

"What did he do?" The words came out harsher than he'd intended.

"He wanted me to have surgery. Implants. To—you know—make me bigger."

Richard instinctively reached out for her, pulling her close. "Was he blind or just stupid?"

"Neither."

"Hell, he must have been both. Kate, don't you have any idea how beautiful you are?"

He feathered a finger across her cheek. Her skin was as soft and smooth and warm as a sundrenched rose.

"When I saw you in that nightgown—my God, Kate, couldn't you see how I wanted you?" Her perfume filled his nostrils, and her eyes glowed like cut jewels.

"Do you still?"

The whispered words broke down all of his self-restraint. He crushed her against him, against the hard proof of his desire, his mouth seeking hers. Her lips were sweet and hot, succulent and hungry, and he couldn't get enough of them. He couldn't get enough of *her*. He wanted more—closer, deeper, warmer, nearer.

Slowly, deliberately, he curved a hand around her breast. She gasped, and for a terrifying second, he thought he'd offended her. And then she arched against him, pressing her breast into his palm. The warmth of her skin through the cotton shirt, her soft, throaty moan of pleasure, the urgent pressure of her hands on his back pulling him closer fired an aching hunger.

He stroked her breast, his thumb rubbing the pebbled peak until she whimpered with desire. She clung to him, her mouth demanding and giving all at once. The kiss was deep and erotic, almost shattering in its intensity.

"I want to see you," he murmured, tugging up her shirt. "I want to see you and touch you and taste your bare skin."

He gazed at her for a long moment, tracing the underside of her breast with his fingertips. "You're beautiful," he murmured, following the path of his fingers with his lips. He claimed her dusky tip with his mouth, tugging and teasing until she cried out, and then moved to the other side and began all over again.

She wrapped her legs around him and rocked against him in a rhythm that set him on fire. He'd never felt so fevered, so eager, so nakedly needy in his life. He'd always prided himself on his self-control, on his ability to make love in a slow, measured manner. He'd always managed to keep his emotions in check, too. Romance had always been superficial and physical, involving his body and mind but never his heart.

But something altogether different was going on here with Kate—something richer and deeper and fuller. He could barely contain himself. He burned to be inside her—but not just to assuage his passion. He wanted to be surrounded by her—encased in her warmth, enveloped in her essence, immersed in the sweet, caring core of her being. It was as if he were seeking his soul, reclaiming a missing part of himself.

It scared him to death.

Abruptly he rolled away. The bed screeched loudly. "Kate—I'm sorry. We shouldn't—I didn't mean—I..." He sat up and shoved his hand through his hair, looking down at her. Her hair splayed out on the pillow like a silk fan. Her lips were kiss-swollen, her eyes large and confused. "I'm sorry. I don't know what happened." He heaved a sigh. "This is a difficult situation."

She touched his arm. "Richard..."

He held up his hand. "Are you okay?"

She nodded.

"Well, then, let's not talk about it. Let's forget it ever happened."

He grabbed a pillow. The bed squealed raucously as he rose from it. "Under the circumstances, I think I'd better spend the rest of the night on the floor. In the bathroom." He strode through the door and closed it firmly behind him, wishing he could close the door on his churning emotions as easily.

Chapter Seven

"You're probably wondering why I sent for you, my dear." Birdie filled a porcelain tea cup with steaming café au lait and handed it to Kate.

Kate smiled nervously, wondering just that. Birdie had buzzed her office a few minutes ago and invited her up to her apartment for coffee. Kate had tried to demur; her emotions were frazzled from the long, sleepless night that had followed that heart-stopping episode with Richard, and trying to act normal around him this morning had stretched her nerves to the breaking point. She hadn't felt up to dealing with Birdie, too.

"I wanted to have a nice private chat with you," said Birdie, pouring herself a cup of coffee, then settling next to Kate on the plump-cushioned sofa.

Kate took a sip of the chicory-laced brew. "What about?"

"Well, my dear, I don't know how to put this delicately, so I'll just dive right in." Birdie set her cup and saucer on a black lacquered Oriental side table and peered at Kate over the rim of her glasses, her blue eyes earnest. "To be quite frank, I'm worried about the state of your marriage."

Kate barely managed to keep from spewing coffee across the room. "M-my marriage?"

"Yes. To be utterly blunt, you and Richard don't seem as, well…" Birdie cleared her throat delicately. "…as *passionate* as a newly married couple should be. After all, by rights, the two of you should still be on your honeymoon."

Kate's hand trembled. Her coffee cup rattled as she placed it in its saucer and carefully set it down on the coffee table. "I'm afraid I don't know what you mean."

Birdie leaned forward. "Richard's spending an inordinate amount of time alone in the office. From what room service tells me, he's even eating most of his meals alone. Why, you two have barely spent any time together since you got married."

"Yes, well, he's very devoted to making the hotel profitable, and he's been working extremely hard.…"

Birdie impatiently waved a multiringed finger. "Yes, yes, I know all that, and I certainly understand and appreciate it. But that doesn't explain what happened last night."

Kate stared at the elderly woman, feeling as if her heartbeat were suspended. *How could she know?* Kate thought wildly. *She couldn't.* Besides, what was to know? Nothing had happened. Well, something had *nearly* happened, but nothing had really occurred—nothing, that is, aside from a kiss that had left her feeling as if she'd had an out-of-body experience, an embrace that had given her goose bumps, and a few caresses that had all but stopped her heart.

She drew in a deep lungful of air and tried to find her voice. When she did, it sounded off-key and breathless. "What do you mean, what happened last night?"

"I'm very familiar with the bed you two shared. You see, Louie and I used to share it when we were first married." Birdie folded her hands in her lap and spoke in a very matter-of-fact manner. "It's very noisy. The slightest movement makes it squeal like a pinched mouse. My room is adjacent to yours, and the walls are rather thin, and, well…" Birdie's gaze was so pointed it pricked. "That bed was awfully quiet last night to be inhabited by a pair of newlyweds."

Kate felt her cheeks scorch.

"Oh, mercy, I didn't mean to upset you." Birdie reached out and patted her hand. "But I can only sell the hotel to a happily married couple, my dear. I do have your best interests at heart, you know. That's why I want to give you this." She leaned forward and plucked a book out of the hodgepodge of items scattered on the coffee table.

Kate stared at the faded gold title embossed on the battered leather cover as Birdie handed it to her. *"Fromby's Guide to Conjugal Bliss?"*

Birdie's long earrings jangled as she nodded. "It's a marriage manual. My mother gave it to me when I married Louie. Her mother had given it to her on her wedding day. My grandmother claimed it made her own marriage heaven on earth."

"I'm touched that you want to loan this to me, Birdie, but…"

"It's not a loan. It's a gift."

"But it's been in your family for three generations!"

"Louie and I were never able to have any children, and I have no one to pass it on to. So I want you to have it, dear."

Guilt squeezed Kate's heart. "Oh, Birdie, I couldn't possibly…"

"I want you to take it, and I want you to follow its advice," she said firmly. "If you'll only do what this book instructs, you and Richard will build bonds of love too strong ever to be broken."

Kate carefully opened the cover. The pages were yellowed and brittle. "This must be very valuable. I don't feel right taking it, Birdie."

"You love Richard, don't you?" Birdie's eyes were frank and direct, and when they locked onto Kate's, she couldn't look away from the old woman's mesmerizing gaze. It was as tenacious as a pit bull's bite and just as hard to shake off. Those wise old eyes worked her over, pulling out the truth like a string on a loose tooth.

"Yes," Kate found herself whispering.

And oh, heaven help her—it was true. She did love him. She'd been in love with him for months. As foolish and hopeless as it was...she was in love with her boss.

"And you want this marriage to last, don't you?" Birdie persisted, still holding Kate hostage with her razor-edged gaze.

"Yes," Kate mumbled, astounded by her own confession but even more amazed at how badly she wanted just that.

But it's impossible, a small inner voice chided. Richard wasn't the marrying type. He'd been burned too badly by his parents' failed marriage. He'd shut himself off from his own emotions. Besides, he prided himself on basing all of his actions on logic, and he had a thousand logical reasons for avoiding marriage.

But he didn't act any too logically last night, the silent voice reminded her. If she'd broken through Richard's defenses once, maybe she could do it again.

She was a fool even to think it, she scolded herself, her optimism disintegrating into despair. He didn't want to be involved, he didn't want a wife and he sure as heck didn't want to be married. It was an open-and-shut case of futility. She was only setting herself up for disappointment. You couldn't make people fall in love against their will.

Could you?

A glimmer of hope sparked inside her. She couldn't keep from clinging to it, even though she knew she was likely to get burned.

Birdie reached over and tapped a pointed pink fingernail on the cover of the book in her lap. "You follow the advice in here, my dear. I don't care how old-fashioned or silly or useless you think it seems, do what it says, and you'll have the marriage you've always dreamed of. I guarantee it." Once again, her blue gaze pierced Kate's soul. "Will you promise me you'll try, dear?"

Kate hesitated. Birdie wouldn't accept a refusal, but she probably wouldn't believe a lie, either. Kate was a terrible liar, and the way the old woman was looking at her, Kate was certain she could see right through her.

There was only one thing to do: agree to Birdie's request—and mean it.

Kate's heart pounded at the thought. How could she agree to follow the advice in a marriage manual that had probably been written before the invention of indoor plumbing? How could she agree to try her best to make a success of her sham of a marriage—a marriage entered into without commitment, a marriage based on deception, a marriage that wasn't a marriage at all?

But how could she not, now that she'd admitted to herself how she really felt about Richard?

She sucked in a long breath, like a diver about to take the plunge. "Okay. I'll try."

"Wonderful." The old woman smiled. "And one more thing. I want you to promise that the two of you will take the weekend off from work and spend some time together. Will you do that, dear?"

Kate nodded numbly, preoccupied by the previous promise, wondering if she were crazy, wondering what she'd just let herself in for, wondering what kind of archaic advice was in the old manual anyway. But most of all, she wondered if there was any chance, any chance at all, that it might actually work.

Richard hung up the phone late in the day and turned to see Kate standing in the doorway of his office. A pang of anxiety shot through him—partly from guilt, because he'd just finished an hour-long conversation with his commercial architect discussing his plans to gut and rebuild the hotel's interior, but also because the mere sight of Kate made his pulse race and his thoughts float as aimlessly as spring pollen. He'd tried to avoid her all day, but to his chagrin, he'd found himself looking for her at every turn.

"Kate," he said, rising from his chair, only to realize as he did how odd the gesture must seem. Kate entered his office twenty or so times a day, and they'd long ago dispensed with male-female protocol.

She looked good. She was wearing a plain blue suit he'd seen dozens of times, but something seemed different about her. He studied her, trying to put his finger on it. He wasn't sure if it was her actual physical appearance, her demeanor or the fact he now knew how her lips tasted, how her breasts felt and how achingly, sweetly responsive she was in his arms.

Stop that, he ordered himself. "I thought you'd left an hour ago." He glanced at his watch, trying to act brisk and businesslike. "It's after seven. What are you doing here still?"

Kate lifted her shoulders. "Unless I want to hang out in Birdie's apartment, I don't have any place to go." She stepped into the room. "How about you? Why are you still in the office?"

He guiltily closed the file folder, not wanting her to catch sight of the blueprints. "Oh, just catching up on a few things."

Kate stopped behind one of the two flame-stitched chairs that faced the heavy oak desk and placed her hands on its back. He gazed at her long fingers with their neat, short nails, remembering how her hands had felt on his back the night before. He swallowed hard. "Is there, uh, something you needed to see me about?"

"As a matter of fact, there is." She gave a slow smile that made his mouth run dry. "Can we talk about it over dinner?"

They both had to eat, he reasoned, trying to quiet the warning signals buzzing through his brain. "Sure." He grabbed his suit jacket off the back of his tall-backed leather desk chair. "Let's go someplace off-property. What's your pleasure—Arnaud's? Antoine's? Commander's Palace? I'm sure the hotel concierge can pull some strings to get us last-minute reservations."

"To tell you the truth, I'd really just like a pizza."

For some reason, her choice pleased him inordinately. "Sounds good. There's a great little place near the French Market. Do you want to walk or take a cab?"

"Let's walk."

The air outside was warm and humid, filled with the rich, earthy scent of the river and the odd perfume of the French Quarter—night jasmine, cooking spices, old buildings and a thousand history-steeped odors that defied classification.

Arthur Winfield met them halfway down the marble stairs outside the hotel's side entrance. "Good evening!" He shook hands with each of them in turn, then glanced sheepishly down at his grease-streaked mechanic's overalls. "I'm just getting off my shift at the garage. I'm not exactly dressed to be seen in your fancy lobby, so I thought I'd try to sneak in the back way."

"Don't worry about that," Kate assured him.

"You're a guest here like everyone else," Richard said.

"Well, I can't thank you enough for all you're doing for us. My wife called me at work and told me you'd located a house for us, and were loaning us the down payment and first month's rent...." The man's Adam's apple moved as he swallowed. His eyes shone with emotion. "I don't know what to say."

From the corner of his eye, Richard saw Kate's stare of amazement. He waved a hand dismissively, wanting to downplay his generosity. "It's no big deal. I called my real-estate agent, and she happened to know of a place you can move into tomorrow."

"I don't know exactly when I'll be able to pay you back, but you can be sure you'll get your money."

Richard shoved his hands into his pockets. "If you'll tune up the hotel limo in your spare time, I'll consider it an even trade."

Winfield's back straightened, and his jaw shifted into a stubborn jut. "That's a mighty kind offer, but I like to pay my own way. I don't take charity."

"And I don't give it. The limo's making more rattling sounds than a haunted house, and I haven't found a mechanic yet who can figure out what's wrong with it. It's nearly useless as it is. If you can keep me from having to buy a new one, I'll consider it a bargain. I'll pay for any necessary parts, of course."

Mr. Winfield's expression softened. "Well, in that case…" He grinned. "My first day off is Saturday. Is that soon enough?"

"That's fine." Richard took Kate's arm to steer her down the stairs. He hesitated two steps down and turned back to Winfield. "There's another way you might be able to help me out."

"You name it, Mr. Chandler."

"Well, I'm remodeling the apartment over my garage, and I need to get rid of some extra furniture—a sofa, some extra beds and mattresses, some of my sister's old baby things. I was going to just have it all hauled away, but if you can use any of it, I can send it to your new place tomorrow."

Winfield's face lit up like a Christmas tree. "That would be terrific, Mr. Chandler!"

Richard nodded as if he'd just closed a favorable deal. "It'll be good to have it out of my way." He took Kate's arm. "Well, I hope you and your family have a good evening. Good night, Arthur."

"G'night, Mr. Chandler!"

The man strode into the hotel as if he were on top of the world. Kate watched the brass door close behind him, then turned to Richard, her eyes narrowed. "You don't have a sister. You don't have a garage apartment. And I'll bet my next paycheck you don't have any extra furniture, either!"

Richard shrugged his shoulders. "Then I'll just have to get some first thing tomorrow morning, won't I?"

Kate's heart leapt, both at the realization of what he was up to and the warmth of his rakish smile. She placed her hands on her hips and tried to eye him sternly, but she couldn't keep from smiling. "There's nothing wrong with the limo, either. I rode in it with Birdie last week, and the engine was smooth as silk!"

Richard's lips turned up in a mischievous grin. "Well, you

never know. Something terrible might just happen to it between now and Saturday.''

Affection, as warm and sweet as melted honey, spread
through Kate's chest as she returned his smile. If she'd had
any doubts of how she felt about this man, they'd all just been
erased. "You're really something, Richard Chandler.''

He quirked up an eyebrow. "Is that good?''

"No.'' She reached up and placed her hand on his cheek.
His five-o'clock shadow rasped deliciously against her fingertips. "It's wonderful.''

He gently caught her wrist, and for a moment, they just
gazed at each other. And in that moment, Kate knew that she
would do anything, anything at all, to win this man's heart.

She stood on tiptoe and pressed a gentle kiss to his jaw. He
gripped her upper arms, emotion flickering across his face, his
eyes clearly saying a peck on the cheek was not nearly enough.
Attraction, compelling and strong, hummed between them—
along with something else, something deeper and more pro-
found.

His eyes were hungry and heavy-lidded, his voice a gruff
growl. "You're playing with fire here.''

"I'm not afraid.''

"You should be.'' His gaze dropped to her lips. She saw
him struggle with himself, felt him stiffen and pull away, knew
the exact moment he'd kicked his wall of resistance back into
place. But even as he drew away from her, she felt a little
thrill of victory, because the fact he felt it necessary to with-
draw spoke volumes about how he actually felt.

"Don't fool yourself, Kate. Just because I did something
nice for that family doesn't mean I'm actually a nice guy.''

"I think you are.''

"Well, you're mistaken.'' He took her arm again and started
walking her down the sidewalk.

"What's so awful about being nice?''

He cut a sideways glance at her, never breaking his stride.
"Nothing. But I know what I am, and I'm not the kind of guy
a woman like you should get involved with.''

She scurried to keep pace with him. "Isn't it a little too late to worry about that?"

"We're not involved. We're just married."

Kate stifled a grin. There was nothing to be gained by pointing out the absurdity of his logic—just as there was nothing to be gained by telling him her heart was set on being both.

"Well, we're going to have to start acting a whole lot more involved around Birdie if you want her to sell you the hotel," she remarked as he marched her toward Jackson Square.

He stopped in midstride and turned toward her, his brows pulled into a worried frown. "She said something to you?"

"She called me in for a little chat while you were at that Tourism Commission meeting this morning. Said she thinks we're not as passionate as we should be. She reminded me she can only sell the hotel to a happily married couple, then she gave me a marriage manual."

"A marriage manual!"

"And she made me promise to follow its advice."

Richard scowled. "What kind of advice?"

Kate hesitated. She'd spent most of the morning poring over the old book, and several of the more interesting recommendations were now affixed with yellow sticky notes so she could easily locate them for in-depth study later. But she wasn't about to tell him about those.

She searched her mind for some of the other, more mundane suggestions. "It says couples should eat meals together, look into each other's eyes when they talk, spend their free time together, hold hands—that sort of thing. And she made me promise we'd take off from work and spend some time together this weekend."

Whew. Richard expelled a breath he hadn't realized he was holding and resumed walking. For a moment there, he'd been afraid Birdie had given her a book that recommended she wrap herself in clear plastic and serve herself up like a ham sandwich. He was having a hard enough time controlling his appetite where she was concerned as it was—especially since last night.

"I guess we have been slacking off in the public-displays-of-affection department," he conceded. "We'll have to make more of an effort when Birdie's around."

"It might not be a bad idea to put some effort into it even when she's not," Kate said mildly. "Just so it can look more natural."

Good grief—that was all he needed.

Or was it? He narrowed his eyes, considering. In his previous relationships, once the novelty wore off, so did the attraction. Maybe he'd been handling this all wrong. Instead of putting so much energy into avoiding Kate, maybe he ought to be fighting this absurd attraction by giving in to it a little. Maybe if he weren't so worried about touching her, he wouldn't be so obsessed with the need to do so.

"In fact, maybe we should practice tonight," she suggested.

"What do you mean?" he asked cautiously.

"Well, it might be good for us to act like we're on a date—just to get the hang of how it feels to act like...you know...a real couple."

It made sense to give it a try, he reasoned. If the forbidden-fruit aspect was removed, the whole situation might be easier to deal with. Besides, if it didn't work out, he could always go back to avoiding her tomorrow.

He reached out and took her hand, trying to ignore the surge of lightning that pulsed up his arm at the contact. She smiled up at him, and he found himself smiling back. "Okay. You're on."

It was funny how easy it was—and the farther they strolled from the hotel, the easier it became. By the time they reached the restaurant, they were joking and teasing and laughing with each other like old times. Maybe, Richard thought, things were finally going to get back to normal.

But then Kate tipped her head up to smile at him as he pulled out her chair, and he spontaneously leaned down to kiss her. He kept it light, barely grazing her mouth, but it was enough to set his whole body to throbbing. He wanted to start with her lips, work his way down to the pulse point of her throat and keep going until he'd picked up where he'd left off last night.

He abruptly seated himself on the other side of the red-and-white checked tablecloth. *Face it, Chandler—things will never get back to normal, because there's nothing normal to return to.* All traces of their old relationship had been burned up by the steady, heady current of attraction that sizzled between them, charging the air, heightening their awareness, electrifying their senses. It was powerful. It was thrilling. It was dangerous.

He had to remember it was dangerous. It was one thing to hold Kate's hand, and something altogether different to kiss her. There was only so far he could take this familiarity-breeds-contempt experiment before it exploded in his face.

They lingered over a bottle of wine and a deep-dish pizza loaded with shrimp and artichokes, then strolled hand-in-hand through the French Quarter. They window-shopped the art galleries and antique shops along Royal Street, meandered among a noisy group of gawking convention delegates on Bourbon Street, then wended their way to Jackson Square, where they stopped to watch mimes and musicians and artists like first-time tourists. They climbed the Mississippi River levee and watched a tanker navigate its way under the lighted arches of the twin bridges, then stopped at a jazz club for a nightcap.

By the time they ended up back at the hotel, their arms were wrapped around each other's waists and it was well after midnight. As they entered the lobby, Richard struggled to remind himself of all the reasons he needed to keep his distance.

She was his secretary. She'd married him as a favor. He would be the lowest form of heel if he took advantage of a situation she'd put herself in on his behalf.

"Evening, Mr. Chandler, Mrs. Chandler," called Charles, wheeling a cart past them as they stepped into a waiting elevator.

The words called up yet another reason to maintain his self-control: making love to Kate would be also be the consummation of their marriage.

He gazed at her as the door slid closed, his mind flashing back to the night before, to the way she'd moved and moaned and felt in his arms. She gave him a slow smile, her eyes filled with heat and infinite possibilities. He swallowed hard.

There were limits to his self-control, and he wasn't sure he could spend the night in the same room with her and maintain what little he had left. From the way she was looking at him, he couldn't bank on the needed restraint coming from Kate's quarter, either. His mouth ran dry at the memory of the shockingly passionate side to her he'd discovered last night.

He dropped his arm and cleared his throat. "Listen, Kate— I'll come in with you to make sure the coast is clear, but if Birdie's asleep, I'm going to clear out and spend the night at my place."

The elevator door opened, but Kate stood still. "Won't we have to wake her up to get into her apartment?"

"No. She gave me a key."

Kate averted her eyes before he could be sure whether he'd actually seen a flicker of disappointment or only imagined it. "What should I tell Birdie in the morning?"

"Tell her I got up before dawn and went for a run."

"She expects us to spend the day together tomorrow," Kate reminded him.

"Well, then, I'll come by for you at nine."

An awkward silence stretched between them as they walked slowly down the hall. He fit the key into the lock and turned it, praying the old woman would be in bed, and breathed a sigh of relief to find the living area dark and empty. He led Kate across the room. His hand was on the doorknob to their bedroom when a light abruptly switched on, blinding him with its brilliance.

Birdie stood in the hallway, wearing a headful of curlers, a bright pink bathrobe and an even brighter smile. "Why, hello there, dears! I thought I heard you come in. Did you have a nice evening?"

Busted, he thought glumly. Remembering what Kate had said earlier about Birdie's suspicions, he drew Kate tightly against his side. "It was wonderful, but it's been a long day and we're both, uh, ready to retire. So if you'll excuse us, we'll see you in the morning."

He hustled Kate through the door, then stood with his back against it, stifling a million silent curses.

Kate's lip curved in amusement. "You look like you expect her to storm the door at any minute," she whispered.

"I wouldn't put it past her."

Kate laughed softly as she turned away. Her gaze fell on the pillow-strewn bed. She covered her mouth with her hand, then stared, round-eyed, at Richard. "Oh, dear heavens. I forgot about the bed!"

How the hell could she have forgotten about it? he thought irritably. It was all he'd been able to think about all day. "Don't worry about it. Since I obviously can't leave, I'll just sleep on the floor again."

"That's not what I meant. I meant I forgot to tell you that Birdie expects to hear the bed squeak."

"She expects *what?*" He stared at her as if she'd lost her senses.

Kate twisted her fingers together. "She and Louie used to share this bed. She knows it's noisy, and she thinks our marriage is in trouble because she didn't hear it squeak last night."

"Why, that meddlesome old…" He clenched his mouth shut to keep from verbalizing the less-than-polite term on the tip of his tongue. His frustration was reaching a breaking point, and this piece of information was the last straw. "Come on. If she wants to hear noise, let's give her something to listen to." He grabbed Kate's hand and pulled her toward the bed.

"Richard—what on earth…"

He threw himself backward onto the mattress, pulling Kate down beside him. The bed groaned loudly. "Oh, baby!" he called out.

Kate raised up on an elbow and stared at him.

Richard rocked from side to side, making the bed creak like a rusty hinge. "Help me out here. We need to teach that nosy old dame a lesson," he whispered urgently. He raised his voice to a loud moan, then called out, "Oh, yes. Yes. Yes!"

To his consternation, Kate burst out laughing.

"Shh!" Richard whispered. "You'll ruin the effect."

"I can't help it," she gasped. "You sound like Meg Ryan in *When Harry Met Sally.*"

He gave her a serious frown. "If you keep laughing, Birdie will think my technique is lousy."

The remark set off more peals of laughter. "And she'd be right," Kate managed, hitting him on the head with a pillow.

The ridiculousness of the situation hit him at the same time. So did the sight of Kate's enchanting mouth, curved up in a contagious grin.

"You want technique? I'll show you technique!" He snatched the pillow from her.

Kate lunged for it. "Oh, no, you don't!"

The fight was on. Pillows flew through the air, only to be seized and flung again amid wild shrieks of laughter, until only one pillow remained on the bed. Kate and Richard wrestled over it like kids, rolling around on the mattress, trying to wrest it from the other's grasp.

"Oomph!" Richard gasped as Kate landed hard on his solar plexus.

Kate's expression grew immediately worried. "Oh, I'm sorry! Are you all right?"

Richard gazed up at her. She was straddling him, her skirt hiked up high on her thighs. Her hair had fallen out of its combs. Instead of being neatly pulled back, a mass of unruly curls now free-floated around her face. She looked adorable and bed-rumpled and eminently desirable. But it was her eyes that held him—soft green eyes full of warmth and concern.

Concern about him. The realization that she was so worried he might be hurt did something funny to his chest. His mind flashed back to another fight, one where fists had flown instead of pillows. He'd been six years old when a neighborhood bully had bloodied his nose. He'd run home, crying, only to have his mother chastise him for getting blood on the carpet and his father punish him for not winning the fight. Neither of them had looked at him like this—as though they really saw him, really cared about him, really wanted to ease his pain.

As a matter of fact, no one had looked at him quite like this ever before. A dry, dusty, unused part of his heart felt as if it had just been given a tall glass of water.

He reached up and feathered a finger across Kate's cheek. When he spoke, his voice was rough and thick. "You didn't hurt me. But I've got to tell you, Kate, you're killing me all the same."

"I'm sorry. I'm probably making it hard for you to breathe." She started to move off him.

His hands tightened on her back, stopping her. "You're making it hard to breathe, all right, but not the way you think."

He watched her expression change, watched her eyes widen and her lips part. He pulled her toward him, watching her all the time. He heard the little hitch in her breath, saw her pupils dilate, watched her lashes flutter just before they closed, just before her lips met his. He felt her small, firm breasts press and flatten against his chest, felt her mouth soften and flower and open, and a shudder chased through him. What he felt was beyond desire, beyond hunger, beyond wanting—it was a soul-deep, aching need.

He craved completion—completion beyond the throbbing of his body, completion he'd never sought before. The very force of his need made him draw back and hold her away.

"Kate." Her eyes seemed to deepen as he said her name. He'd never known a woman so responsive, he thought. His mind flew back to the way she'd responded the night before, and the throbbing in his loins pitched to an almost painful level. He swallowed hard and forced himself to say what his conscience demanded. "Kate—this isn't wise. I don't want to hurt you."

"Then don't stop." Her voice was a breathless, agonizing plea. She fit herself against him, bringing her body into direct alignment with his. The sudden intimacy was exquisite and excruciating. "I'll die if you stop," she whispered, lowering her head, seeking his lips, pulling him into a hot, slow, wet kiss.

She shifted her weight sideways, and he couldn't have stopped if his life depended on it—not when she was unbuttoning his shirt, caressing his chest, strumming her fingers across his flat nipples until they were taut, tender nubs. And certainly not when she reached down and unbuckled his belt.

Holding her tight against him, he rolled her over. "My turn," he murmured, unfastening the top button of her cream-colored silk blouse.

Through a haze of passion, Kate felt the slide of fabric, the chill of air as each button came undone and the blouse fell open. A moment of insecurity shot through her as Richard reached for the hook of her bra, and she felt herself tense.

He seemed to sense it. "You're beautiful. So beautiful," he murmured, trailing kisses across her right breast. "Beautiful here…" He kissed the underside, then slid his mouth to the nipple. "And here…" His lips moved to the center of her chest, to what she'd always considered her inadequate cleavage. "And here." His mouth claimed the peak of her left breast and gave it a delicious, mind-numbing tug that made her moan aloud.

"You make me crazy," he whispered.

He was doing the same to her. Her breath caught, then grew fast and shallow.

He took her hand and guided it down, pressing it against his hard, hot flesh. "See what you do to me."

The feel of him sent her senses into overdrive. Insecurity dissolved into wild, wordless joy. Desire, hot and slick and sweet, became a pulsing ache within her. She gave herself up to the moment and to him, letting all thought melt into feeling, shedding all of her inhibitions as she shed her clothes.

He was a generous and creative lover, kissing and caressing her until she thought she'd scream with need.

This was Richard. This was her husband. And she wanted

him—oh, how she wanted him. She was vaguely surprised to hear herself say so aloud.

"Not just yet," he murmured, his mouth and fingers creating a pleasure that was intense, torturous, exquisite—explosive.

He held her through the aftershocks. She sighed his name, silently adding, *my husband.*

"Now," she begged. "Please."

But still he held back, patiently, slowly bringing her once more to the brink. She was close to toppling over it when he finally leaned over her, his eyes dark with wanting, his pectoral muscles tensed and bunched, his breathing labored. She felt the hard, needy press of his desire against her, at the very place where she was aching, dying of desire herself.

I love you, Richard. Make me your wife, her heart pleaded.

He complied. He filled her soul as he filled her body, taking her heavenward until she was flying, soaring, skyrocketing, until stars burst around her and she shattered, scattering into a million joy-strewn pieces and falling gently back to earth, back to the wondrous sight of Richard over her, in her, a part of her.

And still he held back, even though his features were drawn with strain and his back was slick with sweat. "Come with me," he urged. "Let me take you there again."

"I don't think I can. I mean, I'm not... I've never..."

But he gave her no time to protest. He simply took her. Just as she thought she'd die of pleasure, that she could stand no more, he called her name and clung to her, shuddering, joining her on that dark, far-flung, timeless ride.

Chapter Eight

She awoke the next morning to see sunlight streaming through the bottom of the fringed window shade, but the only sign of Richard was a dent in the pillow beside her. She saw her clothes, neatly folded on the bureau, and smiled. How sweet of him to pick them up and fold them for her, she thought, remembering the abandon with which he'd peeled them off her the night before.

It had been quite a night. Her smile widening, she stretched and hummed like Scarlett O'Hara the morning after Rhett Butler had carried her up the stairs.

But Rhett had behaved like a jerk the next morning. The thought made her sit bolt upright, jump out of bed and scour the room for a note.

A quick search turned up nothing. The bed squawked as Kate sat back down on it, frowning. Richard always left a note for her if she was away from her desk when he left the office. The fact that he was less considerate as her lover than he was as her boss was worrisome.

Kate absently reached for the oversize T-shirt draped on the nightstand and pulled it over her head. Knowing Richard and his fear of commitment, he was probably in a state of denial, trying to backpedal from this new position of intimacy as rapidly as he could.

Well, she couldn't let that happen. Pressing her lips firmly together, she pulled the marriage manual out of the nightstand drawer and thumbed through it, opening it to the first place she'd affixed a marker.

Emotional Climate, stated the chapter heading. Kate leaned back against a pillow and began reading.

> By nature, women tend to be emotionally demonstrative, while men tend to loathe emotional displays, preferring to deal in logic. A wife must learn to curb her excesses of emotionalism so that her husband will not feel uneasy in her company. This is particularly true in new marriages, for even positive emotions, when overdone, can make a man uncomfortable. Drippy, sappy declarations of love or a wife's attempt to elicit such declarations from her spouse has made many a new husband so ill-at-ease that he ends up avoiding his wife altogether.

Kate laid the book facedown on her lap and stared thoughtfully at the wall. Richard hated emotional displays, all right—and he was scared to death of emotional involvement. He'd probably left this morning because he wanted to avoid both.

She'd seen other women throw themselves at him, and she knew how he hated mushy confrontations. He was probably expecting that from her, she thought with a flash of irritation. Knowing Richard, he'd most likely prepared a speech. He might even have several speeches ready—one to deal with whatever mood he found her in. After all, he liked to be prepared for all occasions.

Well, if he thought he was going to get a big, sappy, drippy emotional scene from her, he was sorely mistaken. He wouldn't be able to fault her for behaving illogically. She would be the very picture of calm rationality. She'd act as if nothing at all had happened.

Curving her lips in a pleased smile, she picked the book up again and flipped to the next spot she'd marked with a yellow sticky note.

Conjugal Relations, announced the heading in a large, elaborate scroll.

Frequent conjugal relations are essential to marital harmony. It is the duty of the wife to ensure that her husband's appetite is stoked and sated on a regular basis.

"Sounds more like a potbellied stove than a husband," she muttered.

All the same, there was probably some merit to the advice. But how the heck was she supposed to stoke her husband's appetite if he was sleeping in a separate room? The Winfields were moving to their new home today, which meant she and Richard would be back in their suite this evening.

She flipped to another section of the book, hoping to find more applicable advice.

Common Interests, proclaimed the heading.

The successful marriage is one in which both parties share communal diversions. These can be as simple as taking walks together by a winding brook or as involved as mastering a foreign language.

"I might need to master one just to wade through this book," Kate muttered. She skimmed over a passage of flowery prose and resumed reading on the next page.

The most effective type of activities for a husband and wife to engage in together, aside from the activities of the marital bed, are the altruistic kind. Working together to help those less fortunate softens the hearts of the participants, making them more open and receptive to the needs of their spouse.

Hmm. She was scheduled to volunteer at the SPCA today. If she could talk Richard into coming with her, maybe she could put at least this part of the book's advice into action.

The key to getting him to agree would be to put him on the spot in front of Birdie. She glanced at the alarm clock on the nightstand. She had just thirty minutes to shower, get dressed and come up with a plan.

Richard walked through the door of Birdie's apartment to find Kate and the old woman seated at her lacquered Chinese dining table, laughing and buttering muffins as Birdie told a long, rambling tale about Louie.

His stomach squirmed with uneasiness. He felt like a complete and total cad. He'd betrayed Kate's trust, he'd betrayed their agreement, he'd betrayed his responsibilities as her boss.

He didn't know how she'd react. He was braced for remorse or shame or anger, or all three. He only hoped she didn't pull that dopey female thing of assuming that just because they'd *made* love, they were now *in* love, but just in case, he'd prepared for that, too. He was ready for every conceivable eventuality.

Except to see her smile, give a casual wave and continue chatting with Birdie as if nothing out of the ordinary had happened. And he was completely unprepared to face her in front of the sharp-eyed old woman.

"Come on in, Richard," Birdie called, motioning him with her multiringed hand.

Richard realized he'd been standing in the doorway, staring. He reluctantly jointed them at the table and sat down.

"Did you have a good run?" Kate asked solicitously, pouring a glass of juice and placing it before him.

He nodded. For the life of him, he couldn't tell what she was thinking.

"And did you find some furniture for the Winfields?"

Oh, blast—she hadn't told Birdie about that, had she? The old dame would think he was a softhearted patsy. He'd always believed in presenting a tough, rational, completely nonsentimental image in all business transactions. If he didn't, people might run all over him.

Birdie reached out and patted his hand. "Kate told me what you're doing for that family, and I think it's incredibly sweet."

Sweet. Now there was a word that had never been applied to him before. His father would have called it a sissy word.

The thought of his father made his spine stiffen.

"How did you manage to find furniture so early on Sunday morning?" Birdie asked. "The stores aren't even open yet."

Richard shifted uneasily in his chair. "I have a friend who owns a furniture store. I called him, told him what I needed, made him promise to pull off all the price tags and labels and deliver it in an unmarked truck. He was glad to get the business."

"Well, I think it's wonderful." The elderly woman took a sip of coffee and looked from Richard to Kate over the rim of her cup. "So, what are your plans for today?"

"Well, it's my volunteer day at the animal shelter," Kate said.

"How nice! And Richard's going with you?" She turned her bright, perky eyes on Richard.

He scrambled for an excuse. "Well, I, uh…" Dadblast it. Kate had told him the old woman wanted them to spend the weekend together, but they hadn't gotten around to discussing it last night. They'd been diverted by other things.

Thinking of those things made his mouth go dry. He'd never experienced anything like it in his life. On a scale of one to ten, last night had been a twenty.

"It's so important for newlyweds to spend leisure time together. You know what they say about all work and no play." Birdie's gaze swiveled back to Kate. "I bet they can use an extra hand with all those animals."

Kate nodded. "They're grateful for every volunteer they can

get." She gave Richard a winning smile. "Why don't you come? You'll have lots of fun."

Yeah, right. Playing nursemaid to a bunch of mangy mutts was not his idea of how to spend a productive day, and Richard tried to make each day as productive as possible. But it was in his best interests to let Birdie think he and Kate were a cozy duet. He put his arm around her and gave her a squeeze, his mind plotting out his options. He could drop Kate off at the shelter, spend some time at his other office, then go by and pick her up later. "As long as I'm with you, I'm sure I will."

Birdie beamed. "Sounds like a wonderful way to spend the day. Why, I may even pop by and give a hand myself."

Richard stifled a groan. Just like that, the old woman had him cornered. He plastered on what he hoped would pass for a smile. "I'm sure we'll all have a ball."

Thirty minutes later, he found himself in the car with Kate, alone with her for the first time since he'd left their bed at dawn. The memory sent an unwelcome current of heat racing through him.

Well, here it comes, he thought, bracing himself—the big discussion.

"It's a beautiful day, isn't it?" Kate said brightly, gazing out the side window.

"Yep." It was part of the predictable pattern. Start with an icebreaker, bring up the topic of commitment, progress to a discussion about the future, then degenerate into tears or hysteria or a declaration of love. He'd been through this so many times he knew what would come next.

He angled a glance at her, and was surprised to see that she seemed genuinely engrossed by the passing scenery. "The French Quarter looks so peaceful on Sunday mornings, don't you think?" she remarked. "Lazy and quaint and timeless. I could just drive around staring at it all day."

For the life of him, he didn't know what she found so interesting. Except for a sweat-covered jogger and a tall, gaunt man walking a wiry dog, the street was deserted. It irritated him that she was making small talk when he was so anxious to get this conversation over with. "It looks kind of boring, if you ask me."

"Look up there."

He glanced up where she pointed, to the wrought-iron scrollwork of a balcony across the street. A couple in matching white terry-cloth bathrobes sat in the sunlight, sipping coffee and reading the Sunday newspaper.

"I wonder how many couples have sat on that balcony over the past two hundred years, reading a newspaper just like they are? Can you imagine the stories that must have been read from up there? News about the battle of 1812 and the first paddle wheelers on the Mississippi, stories about the Civil War and yellow fever and changing fashions..."

He had to admit it was an intriguing thought. Funny—left to his own devices, Richard never would have looked up from the street to even see the balcony, much less to have wondered about the people who'd perched on it through the centuries.

What did that say about how he was living his life? That he was simply barreling down the road, his eyes locked firmly on the asphalt, so intent on getting to his next destination that he couldn't enjoy the journey along the way.

He didn't like that image of himself—not at all.

Well, not everyone had time for trivial observations, he thought defensively. He had goals to meet, places to go, business to attend to. In fact, he could ill afford to waste a day messing with a bunch of pets nobody wanted anyway.

Besides, Kate was just stalling, trying to work up her nerve to say what was really on her mind. It was time to take matters into his own hands. "Listen, Kate, about last night..."

"I had a really good time," she said brightly.

A really good time? She made it sound like nothing more than an evening's recreation—like a round of miniature golf or a game of Parcheesi.

"The pizza was wonderful, and I hadn't been to a jazz club in ages," she continued. "And I really enjoyed walking around the Quarter like a tourist."

"I wasn't talking about that. I meant afterward."

"Oh." She blinked calmly, her expression blank and inscrutable. "Well, afterward was nice, too."

Nice. Holy cow. "And that's all you've got to say about it?" he demanded tersely.

Her eyes were wide and innocent. "Why? Do you want to talk about it?"

"Hell, no. But I thought *you'd* want to talk about it."

"Oh."

Just "oh"? That was it? "Well, don't you?" he persisted.

"If you want to talk about it, Richard, I'll be more than happy to." Her voice was calm and modulated, the very voice of reason. By contrast, he sounded like a madman on a rant.

He was bewildered at the ferocity of his own emotions. Why did he suddenly feel so wounded and angry? He was behaving irrationally. He needed to stop it immediately.

He drew a deep breath, trying to calm himself. He'd probably feel better if he went ahead and delivered the speech he'd prepared. "I owe you an apology for my behavior last night. I never meant for things to get so out of hand. I'm very sorry. It won't happen again. And I don't want you to worry that this will affect our working relationship in any way. I've already put it completely out of my mind, and I think you should do the same."

"Okay." Her voice was pleasant, upbeat, perfectly agreeable.

He glanced at her suspiciously. Her teeth flashed in a big smile.

Okay? How the hell could she just say "okay"? She acted as though the whole thing had been nothing at all. Hell, she'd expressed more enthusiasm over the pizza than she had over their lovemaking!

He narrowed his eyes, unsure what to make of it. By rights he should be relieved that she wasn't creating a big scene, but for some reason he didn't feel relieved at all. "So you're okay with things?"

"Sure. Aren't you?"

"Well, of course. Why wouldn't I be? I just said I'd already put it out of my mind, didn't I?"

"Yes, you did." She nodded amiably. "So I guess it's all settled."

But it wasn't settled—not at all. In fact, as the day wore on, the more unsettled Richard became.

Not because Kate was cold or unfriendly or acting odd, he thought, spreading fresh newspaper inside a freshly scoured cage. She wasn't. And that was exactly what bothered him. By all rights, she should be as confused and uneasy as he was. It wasn't normal for her to act as if nothing had happened.

Because something had happened, all right. Plenty had happened whether she chose to acknowledge it or not. He'd never spent a more magnificent night in his life. He kept replaying it in his mind, finding it impossible to reconcile this calm, collected woman cheerfully cleaning out animal cages and treating him with unfailing politeness with the woman who had moaned and writhed beneath him last night.

He longed to grab her, bend her over backward and kiss her halfway into tomorrow just to see if she stayed so cool and unaffected.

"Hey, Katie—ready for a little rub-a-dub-dub?"

Richard looked up to see a tall, muscle-bound man walk up and casually loop his arm around Kate's shoulders. Richard reflexively saw red. He abruptly stood and straightened, only to bump his head on the top of the cage.

To his chagrin, Kate smiled up at the Neanderthal. "I'd love to, George, but I'm breaking in a new volunteer today."

New volunteer? He'd be darned if he'd let her pass him off as nothing more than that.

His head smarting along with his pride, Richard carefully backed out of the cage. "Don't you think you should introduce us, honey?" Without waiting for her to do so, he stuck out his hand and squeezed the man's fingers until he hoped they hurt. "Hello there. I'm Richard Chandler. Kate's husband."

George abruptly dropped his arm from around Kate and stared at her in surprise. "You're married? Since when?"

"Since last weekend. It was pretty sudden."

"Wow—I'll say." George stared at Richard. "Well, uh—congratulations." He turned back to Kate. "Maybe you two want to handle bathing the beasts together."

"Sure."

"Well, you know where everything is. The dogs are waiting in row one when you're ready."

"Thanks."

With a brief nod, George ambled away, scratching his head.

A nerve flexed in Richard's jaw. "I hope I didn't interfere with a little love-in-bloom there."

Kate's eyes flew wide. "With George? He's not interested in me that way."

"Sure looked like it from where I stood."

"He's the assistant director of the shelter. He's friendly to all the volunteers."

"That's funny. He wasn't very friendly to me."

Kate looked at him strangely, a faint smile playing at the corners of her mouth. Too late, Richard realized he was behaving like a jealous oaf.

And he had no right. By the terms of their agreement, the terms that he himself had insisted on, he had no claim to Kate. The marriage was strictly a matter of convenience. *His* convenience. A surge of shame roiled through him, joining the confused maelstrom of emotions churning in his stomach.

He rubbed his jaw, eager to change the subject. "So we're on bath duty, huh? Where do we go?"

"Over this way." Kate led him between rows of yelping dogs to the far end of the building, where a large sink jutted from the wall. She bent and extracted an enormous jug of flea shampoo from the cabinet underneath and set it on the counter.

"Where's our first victim?" Richard asked.

"Over here." Kate headed to a nearby row of cages, unfastened the door on the first one and picked up a mop-haired, scraggly dog that looked like he might be part poodle and part schnauzer.

"It's okay, baby," she crooned to the beast, stroking his head. "We're going to get you nice and clean for your new home."

Richard regarded the creature dubiously as Kate carried him to the sink. "He's got a home to go to?"

Kate nodded. "All of the pets we'll bathe today have already been adopted."

"So why don't the new owners bathe them themselves?"

"Because the animals have to be neutered before they're released. It's the shelter's policy." She turned on the water, checked the temperature with her wrist, then placed the dog in the sink. "We're getting them ready for surgery."

Richard gazed down at the frightened dog. "I'm surprised the shelter lets volunteers handle the animals this way."

"They usually don't." Kate squirted some medicinal-smelling green soap on the dog's back. "But George says I've got a way with animals."

"I'll bet he does," Richard muttered. Kate cast him a curious glance. Too late, Richard realized he sounded ridiculously possessive. He cleared his throat. "So how can I help?"

"Hold this little guy still while I lather him up."

Richard stepped up to the sink. His hipbone bumped against Kate's as he reached in to grab the mutt. He pulled away, only to find his arm brushing against her breast. To his chagrin, a flash of desire surged through him. Good grief, he'd had no idea dog bathing could be such an erotic task.

Conversation. That's what was needed here. "George is right—you've got a knack with animals. Have you always had it?"

"I think it's a by-product of growing up with a menagerie. We were always taking in strays—dogs, cats, even the occasional rabbit." She scrubbed the dog's back. "What about you?"

"Nah. Mom thought pets were a nuisance. Dad didn't have time for his family, much less for an animal."

Kate glanced up at him, her green eyes soft. "What kept your dad so busy?"

"He was a divorce attorney—one of the best in the country." Richard's lip curled into an ironic smile. "If he and my mother had remained on civil terms, she could have been his best client. She's remarried four times—each time to someone wealthier. Right now she's on divorce number five."

"But your dad never remarried?"

"No. As a divorced divorce attorney, he had a pretty jaded view of marriage."

"Had?"

"He died five years ago."

Kate stared at him. It was major piece of information to be learning only now about her own husband. She struggled to hide her surprise. "You must miss him."

Richard shrugged, then gave a single, curt nod. "He died right before I started my own business. I've always regretted that. I wanted him to be proud of me."

"I'm sure he was," Kate said softly.

Richard shook his head, his lips tight. "I hadn't really accomplished anything that met Dad's standards before he died. Dad thought that winning was the only thing that mattered."

"How did he define winning?"

"Oh, you know. Money. Position. Trophies." Richard stared down at the dog. "The first time he really paid any attention to me was when I played quarterback on my junior-high football team. He came to a few of my games." He gazed at the back of the sink, his eyes distant. "Man, was I ever proud, the first time I looked up in the stands and saw my father cheering me on. I dislocated my shoulder and wouldn't tell the coach, because I didn't want to be taken out of the game."

Kate's heart turned over.

"I played football all the way through high school, just because Dad would occasionally come to a game."

Kate suddenly understood Richard's drive for success, his own preoccupation with success and winning. Her throat thickened with emotion. "I didn't even know you liked football," she managed to say.

Richard gave a mirthless smile. "I don't. I never did." He readjusted his grip on the dog. "Fact was, I was a lot better at track and field, but it didn't have the same prestige as football in my old man's estimation." That faraway look returned to his eyes. "I think I made Dad proud when I was named senior class president. I overheard him tell a golf buddy about it, so I guess it made an impression. But he never got to see me start my own business or achieve any real measure of success. It's my biggest regret."

Kate was looking at him with that same warm concern she'd had last night—that look that said *you hurt, I care, let me try to fix it.* And just like last night, it touched a place deep within him, a dark, unused place he hadn't even known he had.

He jerked his eyes away from hers, tightening his grip on the dog. What was he doing, carrying on like this? He hadn't talked about the old man in ages.

He glanced sideways at Kate, deciding it was high time to get the conversation centered on something else. "What about you? Have you got any regrets?"

"Not really."

Not even about last night? It was driving him crazy, not knowing how she felt about it. "Come on," he urged. "Surely there's something you wish you'd done differently."

She carefully sudsed the dog's head. "Well, I guess I regret the fact I haven't finished college. I was taking some night courses in Ohio before I moved, and I intend to sign up at a local college here this fall."

"Why haven't you finished?"

Kate shrugged. "There wasn't enough money for both my brother and me to go to school after my parents died. He only lacked one year toward his degree, and I was just a freshman, so I went to work as a secretary and helped pay his expenses."

She was kind—too kind for her own damn good. He usually considered people like that to be suckers. But oddly enough, he didn't think of Kate that way.

He thought she was wonderful.

A soft, warm, thawing sensation in his chest made him loosen his grip on the dog, and the mongrel nearly bounded out of the sink. Gripping him more firmly, Richard turned him around so Kate could soap his other side. "Well, I sure hope your brother appreciated the sacrifice you made."

"It wasn't a sacrifice. It was a trade-off. He wanted to pay for me to go back to school full-time after he graduated."

"Why didn't you take him up on it?"

Kate shrugged. "He was married, and he had a family to support. That's hard to do on what a missionary earns. I didn't want to be an extra burden." Kate wiped a strand of hair from her eyes with her forearm. "Besides, I liked being on my own, and I'm in no hurry. Finishing college is more of a personal goal than a career one."

"But surely you have some career goals."

"I love being a secretary. My only goal is just to become better at it. I'd like to take some seminars about things that can make me more effective—general business principles, hotel administration, that sort of thing. But I'm basically pretty satisfied."

The concept of being satisfied was as alien to Richard as life on Mars. He couldn't keep from pressing her about it. "But don't you ever think about getting into a career that offers more money and prestige? Don't you want to climb the ladder of success?"

"I make a point of never climbing things that don't have a top floor." She lathered the dog's legs. "Besides, I think I *am* successful. I'm self-supporting, I've got a job I love, I've got some close friends, I manage to make myself useful and I'm learning and growing." She smiled up at Richard. "In fact, I'm learning a lot from you."

Not as much as I'm learning from you. Her whole take on life was a real eye opener.

Well, it was easy for her to be satisfied with life, he rationalized; she hadn't come from a background of wealth and accomplishment. He, on the other hand, had come from a family of privilege. It was normal that he would expect more out of life.

Expect more than what? a silent voice mocked. Which one of them really came from a background of privilege, anyway?

The thought hit with sudden, humbling force. Holy guaca-mole, who was he kidding? Kate was the fortunate one. His family might have had money and position, but Kate's had had something far more valuable. He would have given his right arm for a family like hers, a family where people put the needs of each other before their own and didn't even see it as a sacrifice.

They'd had the kind of love he'd always longed for—love with no balance sheets, no scorecards, no repayment plan or promissory note. He'd heard about love like that, but he'd never seen it up close before. He hadn't even been sure it actually existed.

Well, maybe it existed for people like Kate, he thought, his chest tightening with a funny little ache, but it didn't exist for people like him.

"We're almost finished, little guy. Time to rinse," Kate crooned to the dog, easing him under the faucet.

A sense of loneliness poured over him like water over the dog's back. Despite his wealth, Kate possessed some things he would probably never have—the ability to give and receive love, to enjoy the moment without worrying about more press-ing concerns, to be content and satisfied.

Those were things he'd never thought he'd want, never thought he'd need. He'd always considered them to be senti-mental excuses for self-deluded losers.

But suddenly he wasn't so sure. The more time he spent around Kate, the less sure he was of anything.

"Oh, Kate—there you are. George said I could find you here." An elderly man toting an animal travel case hobbled over.

Kate waved a soapy hand. "Hello, Mr. Vincent. This is my—my boss, Richard Chandler."

Richard felt irrationally disappointed by the introduction,

even though he knew there was no point in making an issue of their temporary marriage. He nodded a greeting to the thin, white-haired man. "Nice to meet you."

"Mr. Vincent volunteers here every weekend," Kate explained. "I occasionally baby-sit his cat, Bootsie, when he goes out of town."

"She's very spoiled," the elderly man explained. "She can't stand to see me paying attention to anyone else, so I can't take her along when I go to visit my family." Mr. Vincent turned to Kate. "As a matter of fact, that's what I wanted to see you about. I promised my granddaughter I'd come visit her this week in Shreveport. Would you mind keeping Bootsie for me?"

"I'd love to, but…" Kate turned toward Richard, her eyes holding a question and a silent plea.

He knew she didn't want to turn the man down. He felt a pang of guilt that he was causing her so many problems. Hell, he thought abruptly, surely a cat wouldn't be any trouble. "No reason you can't that I know of."

Kate's smile warmed him like summer sunshine.

"Then I'd love to," she told the elderly man.

"Wonderful!" Mr. Vincent set the cage on the ground. "I sure do appreciate it. I'll pick her up here next Saturday, if that's all right with you."

"That's fine. I'll drop her off with George. Have a nice trip!"

It's working, Kate thought with delight, angling a glance at Richard as the old man ambled away. Just as the book said— spending time together was softening Richard up. The advice about acting calm and unemotional was working, too, she thought with satisfaction; he'd asked several leading questions, trying to figure out how she felt about last night.

Well, she intended to keep him guessing. And she intended to keep following the advice in the marriage manual.

She couldn't wait to see what it suggested next.

Chapter Nine

"I don't know about this, Annie." Kate turned sideways and stared at her reflection in the dressing room mirror. "It's awfully short."

"It's the perfect length to show off your legs."

"Don't you think it's too tight?"

"I think it's a great fit."

Kate turned around and tugged at the bodice. "What about the neckline? Is it too low?"

"It's just right. And the color is, too," Annie added, anticipating Kate's next objection. "Red is definitely your color."

Kate eyed her reflection dubiously. "But I'm not used to wearing something this flashy."

"It's not flashy. It's gorgeous. What did the book say again?"

Kate sighed. It had been a mistake to tell Annie about the marriage manual and her hopes of using its advice to turn her temporary marriage into a permanent one. Her redheaded friend had seized upon it as her new mission in life.

"Didn't it say a husband needs to be reminded that other men find his wife attractive?"

Kate nodded.

"Well, this dinner tonight at the Grand Regent Hotel is the perfect opportunity to do just that." Annie stepped back and eyed her approvingly. "And this is the perfect dress."

"But it's so...so minimal!"

Annie laughed. "Not nearly as minimal as the dresses worn by those bimbos Richard used to date."

That was true, Kate thought. And the book *did* say that a wife ought to keep her husband's preferences in mind when selecting her clothing. If the women Richard used to escort around town were a yardstick of his tastes, this dress was probably too conservative.

Besides, she needed to do *something* to get his attention. Ever since they'd moved back into their own suite five nights ago, he'd reverted to his earlier pattern of sleeping on the sofa, leaving the apartment before dawn and going out of his way to avoid her whenever they were alone.

The only thing that had changed was that the cat now slept on the sofa with him. It was funny how Bootsie had taken to Richard, Kate reflected with a smile. She'd always considered animals to be a good judge of character, and Bootsie was confirming what Kate had known all along—that under Richard's tough exterior beat a heart of pure gold.

And he guarded it as carefully as Fort Knox, she thought ruefully—hiding it behind thick walls, locking everyone out.

Well, she intended to steal it all the same. He'd been hurt so many times as a child that he must have decided it was safer not to feel at all, but she knew he wasn't nearly as emotionally detached as he pretended. A cold, unfeeling man wouldn't have cared about helping the Winfields, wouldn't sleep with a cat, wouldn't have made love to her as tenderly as he had.

Besides, for him to have made love to her at all meant he was capable of losing control. Maybe, just maybe, this dress would help him lose control again.

"You look great," Annie said, viewing her appraisingly.

"All you need to add is the right attitude and a pair of high heels."

Kate grimaced. "The right attitude would be to wonder why I let you talk me into this."

Annie smiled. "Trust me—you look fantastic. Richard won't know what hit him."

When Kate waltzed out of the bedroom that evening, Richard felt as though he'd been KO'd by an invisible fist. Kate was wearing a slinky red dress cut down to there and up to here that flaunted each and every feminine curve. He froze and stared, slack-jawed. It took him long seconds to finally find his voice. "Did Birdie put you up to this?"

"Up to what?"

"Wearing that dress."

"Is something wrong with it?"

Yeah—the way it reminds me of how you'd look without it.

Her brow puckered in a worried frown that made him override his common sense and rush to reassure her. "You look terrific. But you've got to admit, it's not your usual style."

Kate's features relaxed. She ran a hand through the loose waves of her hair and gave a breezy smile. "I'm a woman of many facets. Maybe this is just one facet you've never seen before."

Oh, he'd seen it, all right. And it had been giving him sleepless nights ever since. He swallowed hard and shifted uneasily. "So this wasn't Birdie's idea?"

"No. Why do you ask?"

"I don't know." He wiped a hand across his jaw. His forehead was breaking a sweat. "I guess I was wondering if she'd said anything more to you about the state of our marriage. If she's—you know—still suspicious."

Kate smiled sweetly. "I think the last night we spent in her guest room convinced her there was nothing to worry about."

Good grief, Richard thought, dragging a handkerchief out of his tuxedo pocket and mopping his brow. How could she bring that up and still look so calm and collected? Every time he thought about it, he needed a cold shower.

Just looking at her in that dress made him need a cold shower. And a cold drink. He stalked to the bar, poured himself a stiff one and downed it in a single gulp.

"Is Birdie going with us?" he asked.

"No. She said she isn't feeling well." Kate's eyes filled with concern. "I'm afraid her heart condition is more serious than she lets on. It's a good thing you're taking over the hotel, so she won't have to worry about it anymore."

Richard shifted guiltily. He wished he could just go ahead and tell Kate the truth about his plans, but he was afraid she'd walk out if he did. And if she walked out, Birdie would never sell the place to him. Still, he hated the idea of misleading Kate. At first he'd been able to rationalize away his concerns, telling himself he was keeping Kate in the dark for her own good. But the more time he spent with her, the more it bothered him. Especially since the other night.

The memory sent a fresh rush of desire surging through him. The thought of spending an entire evening looking at her in that dress suddenly seemed unbearable. He set the glass down hard on the counter. "Listen, Kate, I'm really beat. Maybe we shouldn't go out tonight after all."

Her eyebrows rose in surprise. "But the limo is waiting. And you said the New Orleans Charity Association's annual awards banquet was the perfect place to make some good catering contacts."

It was true. The directors of every major charity would be there tonight, and he hoped to book some of the elaborate balls that many charities staged as fund-raisers. In addition to being a healthy source of revenue, the fund-raisers would showcase the hotel's ballroom to hundreds of wealthy patrons who might in turn book it for other events.

"Of course, if you're really exhausted, I don't mind staying in and spending a quiet evening with you." Kate bent to adjust a stocking, giving him a head-reeling glimpse of both thigh and cleavage.

On second thought, staying here alone with Kate was an even worse idea. He ran a finger around his suddenly too-tight collar. "You're right. We'd better go. Do you have a jacket or wrap or something?"

"I don't think I'll need anything. It's a warm night."

And getting warmer by the minute, Richard thought grimly, holding the door open for her.

In the lobby, Charles tipped his scarlet bellman's cap. "Wow! You look fantastic, Mrs. C!"

Kate flashed a smile. "Thank you, Charles. How's your family?"

"Just fine, thanks."

"Your daughter's feeling better?"

"Much better. The morning sickness has gone away, and she felt the baby kick for the first time yesterday."

"That's wonderful."

Richard took Kate's elbow and steered her through the lobby. "How do you know so much about that bellman's family?"

"I had lunch with him in the employee cafeteria."

Richard frowned in disapproval. "It's a bad idea to get too chummy with the employees."

"Why?"

"They'll take advantage of you."

"Charles would never do that."

"Sure he would. He's buttering you up. Why else do you think he's so friendly?"

She cast him a patient look. "Because he's a nice man. Believe it or not, not everyone has a hidden agenda."

"Oh, no?"

"No. Sometimes people just do things from the heart, without having any particular goal in mind. That's when they're being truest to themselves." The small smile she shot him as she climbed into the limo gave him the eerie sensation that she could see right through him, right through the hard, tough veneer he tried to keep firmly in place, right to all confused feelings bubbling around inside him.

She confused him further as she slid over to make room for him, her dress sliding up to expose a long length of slender thigh. The soft, intoxicating scent of her perfume went straight to his brain, wiping it clean of all coherent thought. As the limo pulled away from the hotel, he clenched his teeth and stared out the window, wondering how he was going to make it through the evening without going stark raving mad.

It was almost as if she was deliberately torturing him. He wanted to order her to stop, but he couldn't put his finger on what, specifically, she was doing, besides crossing her legs in a way that reminded him of how they'd felt wrapped around him and making her pert, perky breasts rise and fall every time she breathed. He couldn't very well demand that she unfold her legs and stop breathing.

"Are you all right?" she asked.

"Fine. Why do you ask?"

"You seem tense."

"I don't know why you'd think that," he said tersely. "I'm completely relaxed." Too late, he realized he was simultaneously tapping his foot on the floorboard and drumming his fingers on the armrest. He abruptly stilled his foot and folded his arms over his chest. "I'm fine. Just fine."

But he wasn't. And as the evening progressed, the tension stretched inside him until he felt like a rubber band about to snap. He watched Kate move about the room, still trying to figure out exactly what it was about her that irritated him so.

It wasn't any one thing, he finally decided. It was *everything*.

For starters, she had no business floating around looking hotter than a straight shot of Tabasco sauce. He was certain every man in the place was following her every move. Richard was accustomed to escorting beautiful women, women that other men openly stared at and admired, but this was different. *This was Kate. This was his wife.* The possessiveness of the thought alarmed him. She was getting under his skin, he thought, cold dread gripping his stomach. He couldn't let it happen. He set his mind to searching out her flaws, looking for something, anything, that might weaken the disturbing, irrational feelings that were rapidly growing inside of him.

Well, he wasn't at all sure he approved of the way she was working the room like a professional lobbyist, he thought with a sullen scowl. She'd exchanged business cards with more than a dozen valuable contacts and had set up three actual appointments for potential clients to come view the hotel's ballroom. Heck, she was better at schmoozing than he was. It was hard to fault her for achieving the very results he'd hoped for, but he wanted to find fault all the same.

He watched her talk with the director of one of the city's largest nonprofit organizations, fuming at the way she tilted her head and smiled in delight at something he said.

Why the heck couldn't she smile at him like that? They'd made love, for heaven's sake—fabulous, mind-blowing, incredible love, and yet she acted as if there was nothing between them besides a congenial working relationship.

Never mind that he'd told her to act that way. How could she actually *do* it? And why the hell couldn't he?

He seethed throughout the evening, and was relieved when the lights dimmed and the awards ceremony began. If he could keep his eyes fixed straight ahead on the stage, he wouldn't be tormented by the sight of her.

And then the master of ceremonies made an unexpected announcement. "When a local family lost everything in a fire and it looked as though they would be forced onto the street, a local business stepped forward to help. This business gave the family a place to stay until they got back on their feet, helped them locate a new home and even gave them financial assistance. It's my privilege to present this year's Most Compassionate Private Business Award to the Honeymoon Hotel—the hotel with heart."

Stunned, Richard stared at Kate as the room thundered with applause. "Go on up and accept the award," she urged.

"You go. It was your idea."

She took his hand. "Let's go together."

Great, just great, Richard thought dourly, traipsing to the stage with Kate. The woman was not only a paragon of virtue, but a public-relations genius as well.

She had no damn business being this wonderful—no business at all. It was at odds with all of his plans. He didn't want to admire her, didn't want to be proud of her, didn't want to care about her...and most certainly didn't want to need her.

The final straw came as they made their way through a crush of well-wishers on their way out the door. As Richard paused to accept the congratulations of yet another acquaintance, a muscle-bound man enfolded Kate in a hearty embrace. A nerve ticked in Richard's jaw as he recognized George from the animal shelter.

Dammit, he'd known when he'd first set eyes on the man that he had the hots for Kate, and now he was all over her like white on rice. His blood boiling, Richard reached out and placed a proprietary hand on Kate's arm. "I hate to break up this cozy little scene, but Kate and I really need to be going."

George stepped back. "I was just congratulating her on winning the award."

"Looked like you were doing a little more than that."

George raised both hands and backed up. "Hey, I didn't mean anything. I was just being friendly."

"Any friendlier and you'd need to be doused with a bucket of cold water." Richard tightened his grip on Kate's arm. "Come on. I'm taking you home."

Kate glared at him as he led her toward the waiting limo. "What on earth is the matter with you?" she demanded. "That was incredibly rude."

"We'll discuss it when we're alone," he said tersely, opening the back door.

The ride back to the hotel passed in tense silence. So did the elevator ride up to the suite and the long walk down the hall. But the moment the door closed behind them, Kate turned on him, her eyes glittering hotly.

"You had no right to embarrass me like that!"

She was right, and he knew it. But the frustration that had

choked him throughout the evening was about to cut off his air supply. "That Neanderthal was all over you," he muttered.

"It was nothing but a friendly hug."

Richard gave a snort. "That was no friendly hug. That was an attempt to cop a feel."

He heard Kate's sharp intake of breath, saw her shoulders pull back and straighten.

"I could tell he had a thing for you that day at the animal shelter," he added.

"That's not true. But even if he did, why should it matter to you?"

"Because..." His hands balled into hard fists. He had no words for the hot emotion churning inside him. It was a volcano about to erupt, a pressure cooker about to blow. Her eyes held a challenge that made something snap inside him.

"Because of this." He hauled her against him, pressing his mouth hard against hers. He'd meant it to be a punishing kiss, but he was suddenly the one in agony.

Kate melted against him, her indignation dissolving into mindless desire. Her lips softened, and he hardened in response. She loved knowing that she did this to him, loved knowing he wanted her. Her satin purse clattered to the floor as she wound her arms around his neck and rose on tiptoe to mold herself against him.

"Kate." Her name was a guttural whisper, half prayer, half plea. His hand roved over her back, caressing the bare skin exposed by the deep vee of her dress, then sliding over the silk. She moaned, and his tongue slipped between her willing lips.

He eased down the strap of her dress, kissing her throat, caressing the swell of her breasts. His eyes held everything she'd ever longed to see. "You're beautiful," Richard breathed. "So very, very beautiful."

And suddenly she felt it—felt beautiful and wanted and loved. And she wanted, she *needed*, to share the fullness of her heart, to tell him how she felt about him. "Richard, I..."

She gasped as he swept her off her feet in a sudden, breathtaking swoop. A thrill chased up her spine as she realized he was carrying her, one hand beneath her knees, the other behind her back, to the sofa. He claimed her lips as he gently set her down. As they came up for air, she tried again. "Richard," she murmured. His beard grazed roughly against her fingertips as she stroked his cheek, gazing into his deep, dark eyes. "Richard, I…"

A terrible, bloodcurdling screech ripped the air.

"Oww!" Richard jerked back, his face a study of pain.

Alarmed, Kate bolted upright. "Bootsie!"

The cat clung to Richard's tuxedo, its back arched, its fur standing on end, its claws dug sharply into the expensive black wool. Richard leapt to his feet and yanked off the jacket. The cat clung to the coat even as Richard flung it to the sofa.

"What's wrong with her?" Richard demanded, standing several paces away. "Rabies? Distemper?"

Kate couldn't suppress a grin. "I think she's jealous."

"Jealous?"

A black-and-white ball of fur emerged from the crumpled jacket and uttered a plaintive wail, then jumped down, stalked toward him and began rubbing against his leg.

"See? She's crazy about you."

"She's crazy, period."

"Did she scratch you?" Straightening her dress, Kate rose and walked toward him. The cat let out a warning hiss as she neared. "It's okay, Bootsie," she crooned.

"It's not okay at all," Richard grumbled.

"Are you hurt? Let me see your back."

Richard turned around.

"Your shirt isn't ripped, and it doesn't look like you're bleeding. But maybe you should take it off and let me check to be sure."

Richard gave a rueful grin. "Under the circumstances, I think the last thing I should do is remove any clothing."

Kate's heart sank. His wall was back up, higher and thicker than ever.

He heaved a sigh, then bent and picked up the cat. "I feel

like strangling this little monster right now, but we both probably ought to thank her. I promised you this wouldn't happen again, and I honestly didn't mean for it to. I don't know what happened.''

Kate tamped down her disappointment enough to muster a wry smile. ''Do you need me to explain it to you?''

Richard gave a sheepish grin. ''You'd better not. It's likely to turn me on even more.''

Kate laughed. He shifted the cat, holding her like a football. ''Look—we both know this is a bad idea.''

''Do we?'' she asked softly.

He gazed at her for a long, troubled moment, his dark eyes somber. ''I don't want to mess up our working relationship.''

There was no point in telling him he already had. Besides, she could tell from the despair in his eyes that he knew it perfectly well.

''I want you to continue to work for me after this whole thing is over,'' he insisted.

There was no way she could go back to simply being his secretary after she'd been his lover, but this was not the time or place for that pronouncement. ''By 'this whole thing,' I assume you mean our marriage.''

''Right. Our—our marriage.'' He seemed to choke on the word. He stared down at the cat, stroking her head. Bootsie purred like the engine of a toy train.

''But there's another reason. I care for you, Kate, and I don't want to hurt you. I know you well enough to know that you're not the kind of woman who's cut out for flings, and that's all I've got to offer. So I think you should just go into that bedroom and close the door. Better yet, I think you'd better lock it behind you. And, Kate…'' He looked up, his eyes filled with longing. The depth of his misery made her heart swell with hope even as it filled with empathy. ''It won't happen again.''

Yes, it will, Kate thought, slipping through the door and

closing it as he'd asked but deliberately leaving it unlocked. Maybe not now, maybe not tonight, but she intended to make sure it happened again. And when it did, it would take more than a jealous cat to keep them apart.

Chapter Ten

A quick glance at the bedside clock the next morning confirmed that Kate had seriously overslept. She threw back the covers, intending to hurriedly dress and race down to the office. Her feet had just touched the floor when she pulled up short.

Why was she getting into such a frenzy? If Richard could do without her in his bed, she thought stubbornly, he could do without her in the office, too—at least until she could formulate some kind of plan. After all, her priority was no longer being his secretary. Her priority was being his wife—now and forever.

She pulled the marriage manual off the nightstand and thumbed through it, opening it to one of the many places she'd marked with a yellow slip of paper. Fire And Ice, proclaimed the chapter heading.

Settling back against the pillows, she read further.

To many a man, undressing his wife is like opening a present. The typical male loves uncovering a mystery. The thrill of discovery is heightened if the wife's outer

garments are prim and proper, but her underclothes are
daringly provocative. The smart wife will cater to her
husband's pleasure in discovering hidden delights.

Sounds like great advice, Kate thought glumly; too bad it
would work only on husbands who *wanted* to disrobe their
wives. Richard seemed determined to keep them both fully
clothed at all times.

Kate set down the book and sighed, her mind playing over
the events of the night before. He'd come close to getting
swept away again, she told herself; surely that was encouraging. Even more important, she was certain she'd seen genuine affection in his eyes.

He cared for her—she knew he did. If she could break
through his wall of reserve just one more time, form just one
more connection the way they had before—body to body, soul
to soul, heart to heart—then surely he'd realize he didn't need
to resist his true feelings any longer.

She needed to seduce him, but she didn't have the nerve to
do it openly. She needed to find a subtle, discreet, ladylike
approach.

The shrill ring of the phone interrupted her thoughts. "Hello
there, dear," piped Birdie's chipper voice through the receiver.
"I want to congratulate you on winning that wonderful award
for the hotel. There's a big article in this morning's newspaper.
I couldn't be more thrilled."

"It was quite a surprise," Kate admitted.

"Yes, indeed. I was just down in your office, and Richard
told me you were sleeping in this morning. Are you feeling
all right?"

"I'm fine. But it was rather a late night." Not just because
of the awards ceremony, either. Kate had spent much of the
night tossing and turning, trying to come up with a way of
winning Richard's heart.

Birdie chortled, obviously giving Kate's reply a different
interpretation. "I take it the marriage manual is helping things
between you two?"

"We've never been closer," Kate said evasively. From the standpoint of living conditions, it was certainly the truth. In other ways they'd never been farther apart, but that was a whole other story.

"I'm so glad, dear." Kate could practically hear Birdie's smile through the phone. "And that's one of the reasons I was calling. I was invited to the grand opening and preview sale of a new lingerie shop on Royal Street at noon today. Heaven knows I don't have any use for that stuff anymore, but the sales flyer looks exquisite, so I wanted to pass it on to you. You'll find it on your desk when you get downstairs."

"Thanks, Birdie. I'll try to check it out."

"You really should, dear. The condition of a wife's underwear is a direct reflection on the condition of her marriage."

"I'll keep that in mind." Smiling, Kate switched the phone to her other ear and switched the conversation to a different topic as well. "How are you feeling today?"

"Better, thank you. But I think I'll just stay in and continue to take it easy today. You and Richard are doing such a splendid job running the hotel, I don't have to worry about it. I can't tell you what a burden that lifts from my shoulders."

"I'm glad, Birdie." And she was. She'd developed a genuine affection for the eccentric old woman. "Well, thanks for telling me about the sale."

"My pleasure, dear."

Placing the phone back in the cradle, Kate picked up the book again and stared at the passage thoughtfully. If she could find a reason that Richard *had* to undress her, the advice might just work after all.

Sudden inspiration struck. *No, she couldn't,* she thought. It was outrageous. It was ridiculous. It would never work.

Would it?

Of course not, she told herself. It would take boldness and daring, and she didn't have that kind of nerve. She simply couldn't.

Could she? Because if she could, Richard just might...

"What have I got to lose?" she asked aloud. She'd already

lost her heart. She'd try just about anything to capture his in return.

It took four days for Kate to put her plan into action. She had to find the right undergarment, locate the right dress to wear over it, and take the cat back to Mr. Vincent. Then she had to find the right opportunity to waylay Richard.

She found it Wednesday evening, after the last of the office staff left for the day. Gathering up her nerve, she entered Richard's office to find him engrossed in the controller's monthly report. She waited until he glanced up. "The chef is trying out some new menu items, and he wants us to sample them," she said. "I told him we'd eat in the hotel restaurant tonight, if that's all right with you."

"Fine. I need about thirty more minutes to finish this report, and then I'll be ready."

"Okay. Well, if you don't need anything further, I think I'll go upstairs and change."

Half an hour later, she reappeared in the doorway, wearing a fitted black dress that fell below midcalf and came up to her neck, gracefully skimming her body, revealing nothing but suggesting everything.

"Ready?" she asked.

Her pulse fluttered as he looked up. He gazed at her, and arousal, as steamy and strong as New Orleans coffee, wafted between them.

"Is that new?" he asked, his voice low.

"Yes."

"I like it."

"Thanks."

Her face grew warm as he stared at her. He finally cleared his throat and looked away. "Well, I guess we should head to the restaurant." He pushed back his chair and rose.

Kate waited until he'd circled the desk before she made her move. "Oh, dear." She clutched her stomach. "I suddenly feel light-headed."

Richard rushed to her side and took her arm. "Are you okay?"

"I feel faint. I think I'm going to..." Just as she'd practiced, Kate gracefully collapsed, careful to fall into his arms.

"Kate!" Richard gingerly lowered her to the floor. She felt him kneel over her, felt him take her hands in his, felt him pat her cheeks. "Kate! What's the matter? Are you okay?"

She slowly opened her eyes and looked at him woozily.

"I'll call an ambulance," he said decisively.

"No! Take me upstairs."

"You need medical attention."

"No, I don't. It's my—my bustier."

"Your *what?*" His gaze traveled over her, as if he were trying to figure out what body part she was referring to.

"Bustier. Merry widow."

He stared at her as if she were speaking Swahili.

"It's like a corset," she explained.

His eyes grew large and incredulous. "You're wearing a *corset?* What the hell for?"

"To look good in this dress."

"Good grief, Kate, you need a corset like I need a brassiere."

It was a struggle not to smile.

"Can you stand up?"

"I don't know."

"Never mind. I'll carry you up the back stairs."

Kate buried her face against his neck, inhaling the faint, woodsy scent of his aftershave as he lifted her and carried her up three flights of stairs.

Outside the suite, he propped her on his leg, extracted a key from his pocket and unlocked the door. He turned the knob, readjusted his grip on her and carried her inside.

"Take me to the bed," she murmured.

Bumping the door closed with his elbow, he strode to the bedroom and gently placed her on the floral comforter. One dim lamp burned on the bureau, suffusing the room with a soft, romantic glow.

"I need you to help me," she murmured.

"How?"

"Help me sit up. Then unfasten my dress."

Holy Toledo. His pulse throbbing in his temple, Richard took her hands and pulled her upright. The memory of how she'd looked naked, how she'd felt under him, gave him an immediate physical reaction. He stepped behind her, his hand shaking as he reached for her zipper.

The silk fell open to reveal something sleek and black and lacy under the dress.

"I'm afraid I'm going to need some help getting this bustier off," she said over her shoulder.

"How the heck did you get it on?"

"I wriggled into it. But I feel so light-headed right now I don't think I can get out of it that way."

Richard was feeling pretty light-headed himself. "What should I do?"

"Help me stand up."

He did as she asked. The dress fell away, revealing a waist-nipping contraption that pushed up her breasts until they threatened to spill over the lacy top. It had long satin garters holding up lace-edged black stockings, and she wore it with a pair of skimpy black panties. The overall effect was old-fashioned and sexy as hell, and it made his heart pound like Thumper's hind leg.

"It's pretty tight," she said in a breathy voice. "I'm having trouble breathing."

"You're not the only one," Richard muttered.

Kate gave a small smile. The temperature in the room seemed to skyrocket.

"Where the hell did you get this, anyway?" he asked gruffly.

"At a shop Birdie told me about."

"What was it—a cross between Victoria's Secret and Miss Kitty's Saloon?"

She gave him that same tantalizing smile. "They specialize

in what they call updated antique undergarments. Do you like it?''

Like it? Did a starving man like looking at a steak dinner, knowing he wasn't supposed to touch it? It was agony and ecstacy, all at the same time. ''It's, uh, very nice.''

''You need to unfasten it for me.''

Richard eyed it warily. ''How do I do that?''

''It has little hooks all along the side.'' She turned slightly and stepped closer, showing him a long row of hooks and eyes.

Richard drew a deep breath and considered his options. If he started at the top, he'd be touching her breasts. On the other hand, if he started at the bottom, he'd be fondling the top of her thigh.

The safest course of action was to start in the middle. His fingers fumbled with the first tiny hook, warm with the heat from her body, for an interminably long time. He thought he felt her tremble, but he couldn't be sure because his own hands were none too steady. He bent closer, attempting to get a better look at the recalcitrant fastener, and her hair brushed against his cheek. A strand dragged across his five-o'clock shadow. The soft texture of it, the scent of her shampoo, the sheer intimacy of the situation made his breath catch. He glanced up and saw her watching him, her eyes heavy-lidded, and his breath caught in his throat. He straightened.

''Kate,'' he said, his voice low and rough as an unpaved road.

''Yes?''

''Honey, there's only so much temptation a man can stand.''

The sultry light in her eyes made his blood pump hard and fast. She gazed at him for a long, throbbing moment. ''I was counting on that.''

Her whispered words raced like an electric shock to every nerve ending in his body. He gulped in a lungful of air and found his voice, although it came out so thick he hardly recognized it as his own. ''Are you seducing me here?''

She stepped closer until her breasts brushed his chest, and looked him straight in the eye. "I'm trying my best."

His self-control snapped, and he was suddenly over the edge, plunging headlong into a dark, swirling vortex of desire. He pulled her against him and claimed her mouth, crushing her breasts against his shirt, reaching down to cup her firm, round bottom and lift her off her feet. She wrapped her legs around him, fitting her pelvis against his.

He groaned at the intimate contact and staggered backward to the bed, still carrying her. She landed astride him. He tried to roll her over, but she pushed him back, straddling him, her hands on his shirt, nimbly unbuttoning it. Her hands splayed against his rough chest hair, her fingers tormenting his flat nipples, then sliding lower to unfasten his belt buckle. When her fingers brushed against his hard, aching flesh, it was almost more than he could stand. He stilled her hand as she reached for his zipper.

Rolling her over, he cupped her breast, kissing the part that spilled over the top of the black bustier, working his tongue under the lace until he found the rigid tip. She moaned as he laved it, then started all over again on the other side. "We still have to get you out of this thing," he murmured.

"The only thing that needs to come off immediately are my panties," she whispered.

Her words incited him, almost unbearably so. Running his hand down her corset-sleeked body, he slipped his finger under the lace-trimmed edge of her silk bikini.

She was ready—so ready that he'd no sooner touched her than she started to shatter.

"I want you," she whispered urgently. "I want you now. I feel like I've wanted you forever."

The words could have come from his own mouth, so closely did they echo the secrets of his heart. All of his life he'd been waiting to feel what he was feeling now—a tender, deep, giving need, a need beyond the demands of his body—and he hadn't even known it. He needed to become one with her. He needed to lose himself in her, for he knew deep inside he would somehow find himself along the way.

He ripped off her panties and shucked his clothes, then leaned back over her. She pulled him down and wrapped her stocking-clad legs around him, and when she drew him inside, he felt reborn. She was all he'd ever needed, all he'd ever wanted, all he'd ever dreamed about in dreams too deep and closely held to ever actually pursue.

He'd finally found the one and only place he'd ever really belonged.

He'd finally found heaven.

He'd finally found home.

Chapter Eleven

Early the next morning, Richard pushed aside the stack of papers he'd been aimlessly shuffling around on his office desk and leaned back in his leather chair.

How could he have done it again?

Against all his resolve, against all his better judgment, against all his best intentions, he'd once again made love to his wife.

His wife. It scared the hell out of him that he kept thinking of Kate in those terms. He wasn't superstitious, but it seemed as if there were something supernatural about those blasted marriage vows. Ever since he'd spoken them, he'd felt differently about her.

Possessive. Protective. Tender. Hungry.

He ran a hand down his face and expelled a harsh breath of air. Was he losing his mind? He almost didn't recognize himself anymore. He suddenly filled with all these wistful, unsettled, illogical feelings—feelings he'd thought he'd squelched at the age of twelve, after his parents had fought at his birthday party and tried to use him as a pawn in their argument, both of them wanting him to choose sides, both of them turning their anger on him when he wouldn't. He'd sworn then that no one would ever hurt him like that again, that he'd never let anyone get close enough, and up until now, he'd kept that promise.

But Kate had somehow gotten through his defenses. He couldn't stop thinking about her. He'd even found himself making business decisions based on her values instead of his own logic-based criteria. Just yesterday, he'd agreed to reduce a front-desk clerk's hours so she could go to night school, even though it meant hiring an additional part-time employee. At Kate's urging, he'd launched an expensive hotelwide recycling program that would cost more money than it saved, and he'd even agreed to donate the hotel's old computers to a school instead of selling them for a profit.

He was losing his killer instincts. He was getting soft. He was hurting the bottom line.

But worst of all, he was hurting Kate.

He shoved back from his desk, hoisting himself to his feet. When they'd made love last night for the second time, he was afraid she'd whispered those three little words, the words he always dreaded hearing, but she'd spoken so softly he wasn't absolutely sure. Far more alarming, he'd gotten so carried away in an uncharacteristic rush of emotion that he'd almost said them himself.

Well, one thing was for sure; the situation had gotten completely out of hand, and he couldn't allow it to go any farther. By her own admission, Kate wanted marriage and children and a home. She believed in love and happily ever after, and he believed fairy-tale endings were only found in storybooks.

He strode to the window and stared out at the French Quarter, his spirits so gray and bleak he was surprised to discover that the sun was shining.

Well, Kate would give up all illusions about loving him once she found out about his plans, he thought grimly. As soon as the sale went through and the property was legally his, the Honeymoon Hotel would become the Executive Edge Inn. His architects' plans called for doing away with the elegant marble lobby that Kate so loved—"wasted space," they called it—and turning it into a series of small conference rooms. The guest floors would be completely gutted and the number of rooms would be doubled by turning the existing spacious suites into small, boxlike units. The antique furnishings would be replaced by standard-issue hotel case goods, and the decor would be standardized throughout.

It was the logical thing to do. It was just good business. And as the hotel's sole owner, it would be well within his rights. It would no longer be Birdie's concern. And since he'd no longer be married to Kate, it wouldn't be any of her business, either.

So why did he feel so lousy about it?

He turned away from the window, finding the light uncomfortably bright in his eyes. What was wrong with him? He'd looked forward to owning this hotel, to making it over, to optimizing its profits, more than he'd looked forward to anything in ages. He'd been working his way up to this for years, and now it was nearly within reach. But instead of the sense of victory he'd anticipated, he felt hollow and jaded and empty.

It was because of Kate, he thought, sinking down in his chair with a sigh. She'd gotten under his skin and thrown his whole world into chaos. He hated feeling this way—about her, about himself, about the state of his life. He didn't think he could carry on like this for ten more days.

He had to get her out of here. Fast. He drummed his fingers on his desktop and thought hard.

A business seminar. She'd said she wanted to take one. Well, by golly, he'd find her one—one held out of town, one that started immediately.

He frowned in concentration, thinking it through. Birdie would be a problem; she'd think it was odd he was sending his new bride away so soon after their wedding. He'd have to come up with a convincing explanation.

Maybe he could take the old woman into his confidence, he mused. He could tell her he'd put Kate's name on a waiting list for a popular seminar as a surprise wedding gift, that a vacancy had opened up at the last minute, and that he needed her help in convincing Kate to go. He'd paint himself as a loving husband sacrificing the pleasure of his wife's company so that she could pursue the education she so badly wanted. Now that Birdie seemed convinced their marriage was on solid footing, she'd probably buy it.

Richard leaned back in his chair, contemplating the plan. While Kate was gone, he could implement stricter employee regulations and get the hotel running more like a money-making business instead of a nonprofit charity. By the time Kate returned, things between them would have cooled down, and only a few days would be left in this ridiculous trial run.

There was a business college in Dallas that offered continuous seminars. He'd attended a few himself. He rifled through his Rolodex, looking for the number.

With any luck, he'd find one that started tomorrow. Better yet, maybe even today.

A few days later, Kate barged into Richard's office without knocking, her eyes blazing. "I need to talk to you, and I need to talk to you now."

Despite his resolve to steel himself against her, his heart lurched at the sight of her. Good heavens, he'd missed her. He'd thought that sending her away would get her off his mind, but just the opposite had happened. Her absence had only highlighted how much he relied on her, how much he depended her, how often he looked for her sweet heart-shaped face, her soft olive eyes. Without his intending for it to happen, Kate had become as essential to him as air and water.

And it frustrated the hell out of him. Birdie had remarked yesterday that he'd been as irritable as a lovesick bear ever since Kate had left, and she was right. He knew he'd been impossible to get along with, and he hated the fact that he was behaving so irrationally. It was completely out of character.

Well, he'd be darned if he'd let Kate know how much he'd missed her. He placed a hand over the telephone receiver he was holding to his ear. "I'm in the middle of an important call. We'll talk tonight."

"This won't wait until tonight. I want to know what happened to Charles, the bellman."

The hotel grapevine was evidently in top form, Richard thought grimly. Kate couldn't have been back from Dallas any more than an hour, and she'd already heard about Charles's dismissal.

"I'll have to get back with you, Felix," Richard said into the phone. He pushed the blueprint of the hotel renovations to the edge of his desk, clicked the phone back into its cradle and rose from the chair, forcing a relaxed smile on his face. "Welcome back. How was the seminar?"

"If you'd bothered to call even once, you'd already know," she retorted. "But don't try to change the subject. I want to know why you fired Charles."

Mercy, she was gorgeous when she was angry. He raked a hand through his hair, rankled that he wanted her in spite of his determination not to. "Your pal Charles was abusing the system. He reported late to work four mornings in a row. He was informed that we'd instituted a new policy of zero tolerance for employee infractions, and he chose to ignore it."

"But I gave him permission to come in late this week. We discussed it before I left."

"So he said. I overrode your decision, and he still came in late." Richard felt himself getting wound up again at the thought of it. "I told you the employees would take advantage of you if you got too close to them, and that's exactly what happened."

Kate's eyes spit fire. "Didn't you even bother to find out *why* he needed some extra time off?"

Richard waved a hand dismissively. "I don't have time to listen to a bunch of sorry excuses. Zero tolerance means just that."

Kate glared at him, her hands on her hips. "For your information, his wife was scheduled for open-heart surgery. She wanted him by her side. But I guess you wouldn't understand that, would you? About a marriage where people truly care about each other and need each other, where they love each other and lean on each other?''

Richard's stomach felt as if he'd just jumped off a ten-story ledge. Good grief—he was a complete and utter jerk. He'd told himself he was implementing a tough, no-nonsense business policy, but the truth was he'd taken his frustration about Kate out on an employee he knew she cared about.

His mouth compressed into a tight line, Richard grabbed the phone and punched in the personnel director's extension. ''Fred, get me the phone number of that bellman we dismissed. I need to call him and offer him his job back. I made a big mistake.''

He hung up to find Kate watching him, her eyes warm. Dammit, she'd already forgiven him. It made him feel even worse than he already did.

''That was big of you,'' she said softly.

He hated how his heart swelled at her approval. He didn't want to care what she thought of him. In fact, it would probably be for the best if she hated him. It would certainly be easier on him, and it would doubtlessly be easier on her as well. He'd always wished he could hate his parents instead of helplessly longing for their love.

He shrugged. ''Under the circumstances, I had no choice.''

''You always have a choice.''

Richard knew she was no longer talking about the bellman. Something shifted and changed between them, like the atmosphere before a summer storm. The room suddenly seemed smaller and warmer, the ceiling lower, the air denser and charged with electricity. ''Why did you send me away?'' she asked softly.

Richard averted his gaze. ''I thought we both needed some space. We were getting too involved.''

Too involved. As if married people could be too involved, Kate thought sadly. The remark was further proof that he didn't take their marriage seriously.

She'd known from the beginning that he didn't, that he only viewed it as a temporary arrangement, as a means to an end.

She'd known it, but during the long, lonely nights in Dallas, she'd hoped—oh, how she'd hoped—that he'd change his mind, that he'd be willing to give their marriage a chance. She knew he didn't believe in marriage, but she knew something else as well: he'd made love to her with his whole heart and soul, not just with his body. Against his will, against all of his intentions to the contrary, he cared for her, and she knew it beyond a doubt.

What she didn't know was whether or not he was willing to admit his feelings and do anything about them. She'd spent a lot of time wondering about it. Richard's fear of commitment was obviously based on a fear of failure. Was there anything she could do to help him overcome it, or was he a hopeless case?

She'd pored over the marriage manual in search of an answer, and she'd only found one relevant piece of advice:

Open communication is the cornerstone of a successful marriage.

Well, she was ready to bare her soul. She was tired of pussyfooting around. She needed to know where she stood. If he refused to open his heart, she would stay through the end of the month for Birdie's sake, but after that, she would resign her job. It hurt too much to see him every day, loving him as she did and knowing he would never allow himself to return her feelings.

She drew a deep, shaky breath, afraid to learn the very thing she needed to know. "So where do we go from here?"

His eyes cut away. "We only have to tough it out for a few more days."

Her heart sank like a steamship anchor. She knew what he meant, but she needed to hear him say it aloud. She didn't want to leave room for any false hopes. She gripped the back of the chair in front of her, bracing herself. "And then what?"

He ran a hand down his face. She'd never seen him look more miserable. "We'll follow our original plan. As soon as the hotel is safely mine, we'll get an annulment."

Her fingers tightened on the back of the chair until her knuckles ached. "There's a problem with that plan, Richard. We no longer have grounds for an annulment."

The pained look on his face broke her heart anew. She couldn't stand the remorse in his eyes, couldn't stand his obvious regret about their lovemaking. *She* didn't regret a moment of it, and she wouldn't deny that it had happened. "You told me when we went into this that I wouldn't have to tell any actual lies. I won't lie about what happened between us."

She'd thought he was going to argue. She should have felt relieved when he gave a slow, single nod, but instead she felt her heart crack all over again. "If that's how you want it, then, we'll get a divorce."

She had promised herself she wouldn't cry, but her eyes swam with tears. "That's not how I want it, Richard."

The hoarse, anguished whisper tore at Richard's heart. "Kate..." He instinctively took a step toward her, wanting to pull her into his arms and comfort her. He stopped himself, realizing that touching her would only make things worse.

Dear God, this was killing him. "Kate, honey—you deserve so much more than I can offer. I couldn't make you happy. And I couldn't stand to make you unhappy."

"Just because you grew up in an unhappy home doesn't mean that's what all marriages are like."

"Maybe not, but that's all I know. You need a man who at least has a clue how to have a good relationship, who understands what commitment and love are all about."

"I've found him."

"No, you haven't."

"You know how important love is, how badly it can hurt if it's not there when you need it." Her heart was in her eyes as she gazed at him. "That's more than a lot of people know.

Marriage is a living, growing thing. It becomes what you make it. The only qualification for it is a willingness to love and be loved, and a willingness to believe it's possible."

Her faith in him made his chest ache. It was so badly misplaced, he thought bitterly. His gaze dropped guiltily to his desk, to the blueprint outlining the changes he intended to make in the hotel, the blueprint he'd been discussing on the phone with his architect when she'd barged into his office. She'd hate him when she learned his true plans for the hotel.

She stepped toward him, and he abruptly reached for the large paper, not wanting her to see it. In his haste, he knocked the plans off the edge of his desk, and the paper plopped at her feet.

She picked it up and glanced at it. "What's this?"

"Nothing." Richard reached out for the blueprints.

But she was already reading the title. "The Executive Edge Inn." She looked up at him, questioningly. "What *is* this?"

His mouth went so dry he couldn't answer. He watched her study the diagram, watched her fingers trace the street names on the boundaries, his heart in his throat.

"Canal Street, Decatur, Iberville—why, that's this location!" She looked up, her eyes puzzled and wary. "What's going on?"

He shrugged, trying hard to keep his cool. "I have a few changes in mind for the hotel."

"What kind of changes?" Her brow wrinkled, she studied the sketch of the lobby.

"Increase the number of rooms, add some meeting space. Position it as a business hotel."

"You intend to change the name? It won't be called the Honeymoon Hotel anymore?"

He struggled to downplay it. "I don't intend to tear it down, Kate. Just renovate the inside, make it more appealing to businesspeople. All I'm going to do is make a few changes that will increase its market value."

"Increase its market value? You mean you intend to sell it?"

He shrugged. "Well, I won't operate it forever."

He watched her expression change from bewilderment to disbelief.

"You're going to gut it, change its name and then sell it? Richard, this will kill Birdie. What you're planning is no better than what the other developers would do."

"The exterior of the building would stay the same. In the long run, I think Birdie will think she made the right decision."

Kate glared at him, disbelief becoming outrage. "You lied to me."

"I didn't. I just kept something from you that I thought you'd be better off not knowing."

"You used me."

"Kate, I never meant to. But you don't always view things logically. You let your feelings influence your judgment, and you tend to wear your heart on your sleeve. That doesn't always work in business. Sometimes, in order to win, it's best not to show your entire hand."

Her eyes snapped, and two bright pink spots blazed on her cheeks. "What exactly are you so intent on winning, Richard? More money? Well, let me tell you something. If you had all the money in the entire world, it still wouldn't be enough. And do you know why? Because money won't fill up that hole in your chest where your heart's supposed to be."

She flung the blueprint on his desk. "I thought I was doing the right thing by helping you. I thought I was protecting Birdie's hotel. But I was wrong." Her voice shook, and tears streamed down her cheeks. "I was evidently wrong about a lot of things." She yanked the wedding ring off her finger, slammed it on his desk, then turned on her heel and started for the door.

Richard grabbed her arm. "Kate—wait."

She shrugged off his touch. "No. I'm leaving. I'm sure you and your logical mind can come up with a nice, logical way to explain my absence to Birdie." She marched to the door, then whipped back around, her hand on the doorknob. "And by the way, in case you have any delusions I'm going to continue working for you…I quit.''

The door reverberated behind her, its hollow thud an echo of the emptiness in his heart.

Thirty minutes later, Richard sat at his desk, twirling a pencil and staring blankly at the door Kate had slammed as she left. The logical thing to do was to get busy and figure out a way to salvage the situation, he thought glumly. He should be working on an explanation to cover Kate's absence. At the very least, he should be diverting Birdie in order to keep her from encountering Kate as she stormed out of the building.

But he didn't have the heart for it. He was about to lose the hotel just as he nearly had it within his grasp, but it suddenly didn't matter.

He'd already lost Kate. And too late, he realized she was all he really wanted.

He thought about life without her, and his spirits sagged even farther. He'd missed so many things about her during the few days she'd been away at the seminar—the way she brightened his day when she walked into the room, the way her eyes lit up when she smiled, the soft, breathy way she called his name when they made love….

The pencil snapped in two in his hand. Maybe she hadn't left yet. If he hurried, maybe he could still catch her. He had no idea what he would say to her or how he would make her stay. He only knew he couldn't let her leave.

He took the back stairs, sprinting up them two at a time. His pulse pounded as he turned the key in the door.

She was gone. He sensed her absence the minute he stepped into the suite, but he checked the bedroom anyway. His heart sank at the sight of the empty closet, the bare bathroom counter.

Gone. She was gone.

He knew it beyond a doubt when he saw her gold wedding band glimmering on the bedroom bureau. He picked it up. The ring felt hard and cold against his palm. Slipping it in his pocket, he turned to gaze out the window, his heart as empty as the deserted room.

An elderly couple strolled along the street, their arms entwined, their gray heads bent together, laughing. He recognized them as hotel guests celebrating their fiftieth wedding anniversary. He remembered them because they'd requested a special suite, and he'd had to relocate another couple to accommodate them.

They sure didn't fit his image of a bored, long-suffering married couple. Come to think of it, none of the other hotel guests did, either. As a matter of fact, now that he honestly thought about it, he couldn't think of a single married couple who looked as miserable as he felt.

Dammit, he hadn't only been lying to Birdie; he'd been lying to himself. He'd wanted to believe that the whole institution of marriage was flawed, when in truth the flaw was within himself.

He didn't really think marriage was a bad risk. He thought he was.

He wasn't afraid of commitment. He was afraid of failing at it.

He propped both hands against the window frame and stared down, processing the insight. It really didn't change anything, he thought glumly. Kate still deserved better.

And she'd no doubt find it. The thought sent a sharp ache through his chest. She might think she loved him now, but in a few months she'd probably fall in love with someone else. In his experience, love was a pretty transient state of affairs. Women were always claiming to be in love with him. His own mother had remarried five times.

But he'd never felt like this before. He'd never felt *anything* like this before.

The couple on the sidewalk stopped and kissed. Richard turned away, the tender scene stabbing at his heart like an ice pick at a wound.

He was halfway across the room when something caught the corner of his eye. He glanced over and saw an old book sitting on top of the bedroom trash can, bright yellow notes sticking out from the pages. Curious, he strode over and picked it up.

Fromby's Guide to Conjugal Bliss. He riffled through it, glancing at the notes.

His heart raced as he recognized Kate's handwriting. She'd told him Birdie had given her an old marriage manual, but she hadn't told him she'd been following its advice. He sank down heavily on the bed, the depth of Kate's caring striking him like a blow.

Kate was a forever kind of woman. She didn't take love lightly, and she wouldn't give it that way, either. She wasn't a bimbo looking for a meal ticket or a trophy husband. She was the kindest, warmest, most decent human being he'd ever met, and she'd done everything in her power to try to win his heart. She loved him. She really loved him, in that whole-hearted, unconditional, just-as-you-are, flaws-and-all kind of way that he'd always wanted to be loved.

And he loved her. How could he not? The only wonder was why it had taken him so long to realize it.

He could trust his heart to Kate. He instinctively, unequivocally knew that. But could she trust hers to him?

He gazed down at the worn, well-thumbed book, the pages ruffled with yellow notes that Kate had made as she'd thought about him, and he knew the answer.

Yes. He would become the man she deserved—the man she'd thought he was.

The first thing he needed to do was to level with Birdie. If it meant losing the hotel, then so be it. By losing the hotel, he might have another chance at winning the only thing that really mattered.

Richard sat back in the faux-leopard-skin-covered Louis XIV chair in Birdie's living room an hour later, relieved to be at the end of his arduous confession. "So there you have it," he said with a sigh. His eyebrows lifted at the old woman's serene expression. "You don't look all that surprised."

Birdie shrugged. "Well, I wasn't born yesterday. I knew you and Kate weren't really engaged the first time you came to see me."

"You did?" Richard sat forward. "So why did you push us to get married?"

"I'm an old matchmaker at heart. In fact, that's going to be my new profession. When I sell the hotel, I'm going to open a dating service."

"But if you knew we weren't engaged, then why...?"

Birdie smiled. "When you were willing to go through with it, I thought to myself, Now there's a man who's passionate about the hotel. And when I saw the way Kate looked at you, I thought, Now there's a woman who really loves that man. All that remained to be seen was whether you were smart enough to recognize a good thing when you had it." Birdie folded her hands in her lap and batted her false eyelashes. "Louie always said I had sound instincts about people, and I could tell you'd be good for each other."

Richard shook his head. "It's pretty obvious that Kate is good for me, but I'm not so sure I'm good for Kate."

"Of course you are. You're perfect. You keep her grounded, like my Louie kept me. She's so softhearted that every Tom, Dick and Harry with a halfway plausible sob story would take advantage of her otherwise."

"So you're not angry with me?"

"I would have been if you hadn't come clean. But since you have..." She lifted her shoulder, smiled and took a sip of sherry. "You know, I really don't have a problem with most of your plans."

Richard felt as if he needed to pick his jaw off the floor. "You don't?"

"No. I know progress is inevitable. Of course, I think you should preserve at least a part of the lobby, and I do think you should keep one or two floors of honeymoon suites so our former guests will have a romantic place to return to, but I understand the need to be competitive in today's market."

Richard stared at her, his mind reeling. "I don't understand,

Birdie. If you're so agreeable to change, why did you insist on the trial run?''

She reached out and patted his cheek. ''All Louie and I ever wanted was for the hotel to be filled with love. That was the thing I needed to be sure of. And with you and Kate running it, it will be.''

''You're assuming I can win her back. I'm not so sure I can.''

''Of course you can. It'll be easy. All you have to do is figure out what she wants more than anything in the world, then give it to her.''

''That's easy?''

''Easy as pie.''

''I've never made a pie in my life.'' He gazed earnestly at Birdie. ''Will you help me?''

The old woman beamed. ''I'd like nothing more.''

Kate leaned on the mop and stared glumly around her immaculate apartment. She'd scoured it from floor to ceiling since she'd come home five hours ago, needing to do something, anything, to work off her anger at Richard. By and large, it had worked. She no longer felt angry.

She simply felt empty.

Angry was better, Kate thought, heaving a sigh as she rinsed out the mop in the kitchen sink. Anything was better than this cold, aching loneliness.

How could she have been so wrong about Richard? She'd trusted him, and he'd betrayed her.

No, she thought morosely; she'd betrayed herself. She'd fallen in love with the least likely marriage prospect she could find.

She wrung out the mop with a vengeance, castigating herself for such an unforgivable lapse in judgment. She'd always been clear about what she wanted. She'd always made a point of not dating men who weren't good matrimonial prospects. But Richard had stolen her heart before she'd even realized what was happening. She'd fallen hard and fast, head over heels. From the moment she'd met him, no other man had held any appeal.

And the sad, horrible fact was that she feared no other man ever would.

Tears clouded her eyes, and she tried to blink them away. She didn't want to give in to her emotions. If she gave in to them, they might just overwhelm her, and she needed a clear head to figure out a plan of action. She needed to decide if she was going to stay in New Orleans or move back to Ohio. She needed to find a new job. She needed to find a way to make it through the rest of her life without the man to whom she'd completely, irrevocably given her heart.

The ring of the telephone intruded on her thoughts. Kate crossed the room and answered it. "Katie, dear," said a faint voice.

"Birdie?" Kate was instantly alarmed. The elderly woman didn't sound at all like herself. "Are you all right?"

"Richard told me what happened. He told me everything— how you two got married so he could buy the hotel, how you're planning a divorce. He told me the whole story."

"He did?" The information stunned Kate. She'd been certain Richard would have figured out a way to explain her absence without giving away the truth.

"Yes. And I must say, it was quite a shock."

Oh, dear, Kate thought anxiously—Birdie's heart condition. A shock like this could be devastating. Kate's fingers tightened on the phone. "Are you all right?"

"I—I think I might need some help."

"I'll call 911," Kate said quickly.

"No, no, dear. I won't go to a hospital unless I'm already unconscious. But would you mind coming over here?"

Guilt, responsibility, remorse and concern all rushed through Kate at once. She'd never refused a plea for help in her life, and she wasn't about to start now. "I'll be right there."

Kate drove up to the front entrance of the hotel and braked hard, the tires of her small car screeching to a stop. As a bellman opened her door, she looked up to see a familiar smiling face.

"Charles. You're back!"

"Yes, ma'am. Mr. Chandler came by the hospital this afternoon. He brought flowers to my wife and apologized to me, and asked if I could come back to work right away. He even offered me a nice raise. So here I am."

Richard had taken time from work to go by the hospital, visit a woman he didn't know and apologize to an employee? Kate tried to steel herself against the rush of warm emotion, but it was too late. Her heart was touched, and it ached anew. "I'm so sorry about what happened. I should have explained your situation to Mr. Chandler before I left town."

Charles shrugged. "It was all a misunderstanding. Everything's fine now."

"Your wife's surgery went well?"

He nodded. "The doctors say she'll be good as new."

"I'm so glad." Kate scrambled out of her car, hoping the same could be said about Birdie. Her brow furrowed with worry at the thought. "Do you know how Birdie's doing? She just called me and she didn't sound well at all."

Charles shook his grizzled head. "All I know is she called the bellstand and asked me to send you up to the top floor as soon as you arrived."

Kate hurried inside. The elevator seemed maddeningly slow. When it finally opened on the sixth floor, she saw Birdie standing at the end of the hall, clad in her usual shade of parrot pink.

Kate dashed toward her, wondering why the woman was loitering in the hallway instead of resting in her apartment at the opposite end of the hall. "Birdie! Are you all right? What are you doing here?"

"Why, I was waiting for you, dear."

"You sounded terrible on the phone. I was worried sick about you! Is your heart all right?"

Birdie gave a sly smile. "Mine is fine, but someone else

here is having heart trouble.'' She opened a door and gave Kate a gentle push. "Go on in and see if you can help, dear.''

Before she knew it, Kate found herself in a dimly lit room filled with fresh flowers and soft music, a room that looked strangely familiar. "Birdie, what on earth..." She turned around just as Birdie left the room, closing the door firmly behind her.

Confused, Kate swiveled back around. Her heart lurched. Oh, dear—it was the suite where she and Richard had spent their wedding night. And there he was, walking toward her out of the shadows at the far end of the room, with something in his hand.

Her traitorous heart pounded madly. She hated herself for reacting to him this way. She lifted her chin, determined not to let him know how he affected her, not to let him get the best of her. "I don't know what you're up to, Richard, but I won't help you pull another fast one on Birdie.''

"I'm not trying to pull a fast one. I told her everything.''

"You mean you told her a fresh pack of lies to explain away the old ones?''

"No. I mean I told her the complete and total truth.''

Birdie had said as much on the phone. Kate stared at him, trying to make sense of it all, trying to steel her heart against further injury, but her pulse raced as he stepped toward her.

"But first I had to face the truth myself.''

She should leave, Kate told herself. She was only giving him another chance to hurt her again. She knew she should walk out the door and not look back, but her feet seemed set in concrete.

"I've got more baggage to deal with than a whole crew of bellmen,'' he confessed. "But instead of dealing with it, I've been trying to hide from it. My dad made me feel like such a loser if I ever made a mistake that I started avoiding situations where I felt like I was at a disadvantage. Serious relationships seemed like the worst risk of all, so I avoided ever getting involved in one.''

He took another step toward her, his dark eyes somber. "I

tried telling myself that love didn't matter or even really exist. And then you came along, and I couldn't pretend to believe that anymore." He stepped closer, regretfully shaking his head. "I've been a fool, Kate. A complete and utter fool. I've been thinking a lot about what you said, and you were right. No amount of money or success will ever fill up the hole in my heart. But I've found something that will."

Kate's voice was little more than a whisper. "What?"

"You."

Kate's heart took off like an untethered balloon, rising and soaring, high and free.

"I love you, Kate, and I want to be the kind of man you can love in return. I've even found a book that I hope can help." He held up a familiar leatherbound volume.

"Birdie's marriage manual," Kate whispered.

Richard nodded. "I've been reading the instructions for husbands." He flipped it open to a page marked by a paper clip and read aloud. "'The wise husband strives to create a sense of romance. Women love to be continually wooed by candlelight and roses.'" He looked up and grinned. "I thought I'd give it a try. Just for good measure, I added soft music and champagne. Would you like a glass?"

Kate shook her head. She already felt as if she'd had way too much to drink, and she hadn't touched a drop.

"I know I've been an insensitive dolt, so I looked up the section on how to make up after an argument." He flipped to another page. "'An unexpected gift, carefully selected to delight your wife, will go a long way toward mending broken fences.'" He looked up and gave a sheepish grin. "I hope you like what I got for you. It seemed like a good idea at the time."

He left the room, only to return a moment later with a large box covered with a loose-fitting lid. "I'll hold the box while you open it."

Dumbstruck, Kate raised the top. A tiny white kitten with an enormous red satin bow around its neck looked up and mewed.

Kate's heart turned over. She gazed up at Richard, then lifted the kitten from the box. "Oh, he's adorable!"

"It's a she. I told George at the animal shelter that I'm not about to share you with another male. He laughed and said he didn't blame me. And he accepted my apology for acting like a jerk the other night. Oh, and by the way—we're both scheduled for volunteer duty next weekend."

Richard had gone to the animal shelter to apologize to George and get her a pet—*and* he'd signed up for volunteer duty?

He grinned, his eyes warm. "Hopefully this cat is young enough to get accustomed to sharing my affections, so there won't be any more jealous interruptions like we had with Bootsie."

Kate cradled the kitten and gazed at Richard, unable to process it all. Her heart felt as if it were about burst, yet a tiny protective part held back, afraid to trust him, afraid to give in to the swelling sense of joy. What if this was just a new, more convincing ploy to get the hotel? "Richard, I don't know if…"

He placed a finger to her lip. "Please, hear me out before you say anything."

His eyes were dark and earnest and imploring. Wordlessly, Kate nodded.

Richard took the kitten from her arms and gently set it on the floor. When he straightened, he placed the book on the sofa, stepped close and took both of Kate's hands in his. "The manual had another piece of advice I think I need to follow. It said a husband should tell his wife how he feels about her. I'm not very good at this sort of thing, but I want to give it my best shot."

He drew a deep breath. Kate saw his throat convulse as he swallowed. "I love you. When you walked out today, I realized that nothing means anything without you. It suddenly didn't matter if I lost the hotel and everything I own or gained the whole world. I knew that in order to stand a prayer of winning you back, I needed to show you I was willing to change. So I went to Birdie and confessed. I thought she was going to say the deal was off, but I didn't care. I only cared about getting you back.''

He'd been willing to give up the hotel—the thing he wanted more than anything else in the world—in order to win her back. Her knees wobbled, her head reeled, her heart spun and danced and sang and soared.

He pulled something out of his pocket. Kate saw it glitter in the dim light, and realized it was the gold band he'd placed on her finger at their wedding. ''I want to marry you again, Kate. I know we're already married, but I want to say those vows to you knowing that I mean them, and I want to hear them from you the same way.''

Kate's eyes filled with tears.

His gaze was warm and caring and desperately earnest. ''I want you to be my wife—my real wife, my forever wife, my love-of-my-life wife. I promise always to love you, always to be faithful to you, to put you before work or money or anything else. If you'll just say yes, I promise to devote the rest of my life to making you happy.''

Kate's eyes felt as full as her heart. ''Oh, Richard—you already have,'' she whispered. ''If I were any happier, I think my heart would burst.''

He pulled her into his arms. When their lips met, she felt as if their souls touched as well. The kiss was deep and consuming, full of both longing and promise.

Long, breathless moments later, he drew back and gave her a tender smile. ''That book's advice seems to work pretty well. Maybe I ought to consult it to see what to do next.''

Kate grinned up at him. ''You don't need a book to know what your next move should be,'' she whispered, pulling his head back down.

''I guess you're right at that,'' he murmured, bending to reclaim her lips.

* * * * *

A good one isn't hard to find—they're right here in Silhouette Romance!

MAN: Vincent Pastorelli, Committed Fireman

Look out for the woman who melts Vincent's
heart in Carla Cassidy's
WILL YOU GIVE MY MOMMY A BABY? (August 1998)

MAN: Alex Trent, Wealthy Businessman

Find out how Alex convinces his best friend to
open her heart in Christine Scott's
HER BEST MAN (September 1998)

MAN: Devin Bartlett, 100% Cowboy

Meet the woman who will make Devin commit
once again in Robin Nicholas's
COWBOY DAD (October 1998)

Available at your favorite retail outlet.

Silhouette ROMANCE™

The World's Most Eligible Bachelors are about to be named! And Silhouette Books brings them to you in an all-new, original series....

World's Most
Eligible Bachelors

Twelve of the sexiest, most sought-after men share every intimate detail of their lives in twelve never-before-published novels by the genre's top authors.

Don't miss these unforgettable stories by:

Dixie Browning

Marie Ferrarella

Jackie Merritt

Tracy Sinclair

BJ James

RACHEL LEE   Suzanne Carey

Gina Wilkins

VICTORIA PADE

MAGGIE SHAYNE   *Anne McAllister*

Susan Mallery

Look for one new book each month in the
World's Most Eligible Bachelors series beginning
September 1998 from Silhouette Books.

V™ *Silhouette* ®

Available at your favorite retail outlet.

MATERNITY LEAVE

Coming September 1998

Three delightful stories about the blessings
and surprises of "Labor" Day.

TABLOID BABY by Candace Camp

She was whisked to the hospital in the nick of time....

THE NINE-MONTH KNIGHT
by Cait London

A down-on-her-luck secretary is experiencing
odd little midnight cravings....

THE PATERNITY TEST by Sherryl Woods

The stick turned blue before her
biological clock struck twelve....

*These three special women are very pregnant...and very
single, although they won't be either for too much longer,
because baby—and Daddy—are on their way!*

Available at your favorite retail outlet.

HERE COME THE
Virgin Brides!

Celebrate the joys of first love with more unforgettable stories from Romance's brightest stars:

SWEET BRIDE OF REVENGE
by Suzanne Carey—June 1998 (SR #1300)

Reader favorite Suzanne Carey weaves a sensuously powerful tale about a man who forces the daughter of his enemy to be his bride of revenge. But what happens when this hard-hearted husband falls head over heels...for his wife?

THE BOUNTY HUNTER'S BRIDE
by Sandra Steffen—July 1998 (SR #1306)

In this provocative page-turner by beloved author Sandra Steffen, a shotgun wedding is only the beginning when an injured bounty hunter and the sweet seductress who'd nursed him to health are discovered in a remote mountain cabin by her gun-toting dad and *four* brothers!

SUDDENLY...MARRIAGE!
by Marie Ferrarella—August 1998 (SR #1312)

RITA Award-winning author Marie Ferrarella weaves a magical story set in sultry New Orleans about two people determined to remain single who exchange vows in a mock ceremony during Mardi Gras, only to learn their bogus marriage is the real thing....

And look for more VIRGIN BRIDES in future months, only in—

Silhouette ROMANCE™

Available at your favorite retail outlet.

Look us up on-line at: http://www.romance.net   SRVBJ-A